Trapstar 2

"Trapping Aint Dead"

By Blake Karrington

Trapstar 2

Contents

Chapter 1

The sky was blanketed in midnight blue as the black on black Ford F150 eased towards the house. Brianna sat in the passenger seat of Kacy's truck with her thighs on her hands attempting to hide the nervous energy that made them tremble. Brianna wasn't used to being on this side of the game. She'd felt at ease being behind the scene, doing all the things that kept her hands clean. But things had changed almost immediately after Hakeem's arrest. Not only was there more money to be made, but there was definitely more money to be collected. There was no way should could afford to not collect on 20 kilos of dope. That was the one thing that she hadn't factored into the equation when she had plotted to set up Hakeem. While Brianna was satisfied that her revenge on him had been sufficient, she'd forgotten that he'd been somewhat of an ally when it came to her business. There was no time to sit around and mull over the details of this discrepancy. Instead she had to act, and she had to act fast.

Kacy looked over at her and asked, "You aiight?"

"I'm just ready to get this over with." Brianna said.

"Ok." He said as he eased around the corner and turned his headlights off. "I know Tre had to prepare you for this type of battle."

Brianna nodded, "He did... I just never thought I'd have to use it."

"Well... it's time to see what you're made of."

Kacy and Brianna got out of the car and walked to the door of the one story ranch house. They could hear a TV blaring from the porch, and saw lights on. Kacy stepped up to the door and slammed the side of his fist onto the door three times. Almost immediately the TV went silent, and the door cracked open. Kacy kicked the door the rest of the way open with his size twelve boots. Everyone inside began running. Kacy let off two shots into the wall. They all froze.

"All you niggas get on the couch". He motion with the twelve gauge shot gun. As the four men sat on the couch Brianna began to speak.

"Look mutha-fuckas, it seems to be some misunderstanding on who to pay since Havoc is away. Well let me help you get this shit right. Who is Big D?"

Instantly, three of the men looked in the direction of the short heavyset man on the left end of the sofa. Brianna walked up and stood right in front of him.

"Put your hands on your knees Nigga."

Big D placed both his hands on his knees, and looked up at Brianna with a nervous stare.

"Now Big D where is my money?"

"Tiffany already came and picked it up. Hakeem called me from the joint and told me to give it to her! Look I didn't know anything different so that's what I did."

"Nigga you gave that bitch my money?"

"Not all of it, there's $85,000.00 in the backroom."

Kacy motioned to one of the other guys, to go to the backroom and get the money. He followed behind the man closely, until he pulled the money bag out the closet. When they entered back into the living room he gave Brianna a heads up look. She was still standing over Big D.

She asked him, "Which hand you whip the dope up with?"

"Huh?" Big D looked confused.

"Which hand you cook with nigga? I don't want to put you out of work?" Big D still looked confused.

"Fuck it!" Brianna said as she placed the gun on top of his left hand and pulled the trigger!

"Got Damit!!!" Big D hollered.

"Nigga, now you will know the next time you hand my money

to someone, that will be a hand you lose!" She turned around and walked towards the door.

"Oh yea, you nigga's be prepared, we got some work coming in next week. Anybody got a problem with working for me?"

All the men shook their heads no. Brianna turned and walked out the house.

She and Kacy got back in the truck, money and respect in tow.

Kacy smiled at Brianna, "I didn't know you had it in you."

Brianna laughed, "Like the saying goes... don't judge a book by its cover."

Just as they made it out of the neighborhood, Brianna felt a familiar feeling bubbling up in her belly.

"Pull over."

"Now?" Kacy said confused.

"Now!"

As soon as Kacy stopped the car, Brianna slung the door open, got out and vomited all over the pavement.

"Damn!" Kacy shouted.

Brianna wiped her mouth with the back of her hand and stumbled the couple steps back to the car.

Kacy sat there with a grin on his face, "I guess you're not as tough as we thought you were."

Brianna shook her head, "No, it's not that. I think I have a bug or something. Been throwing up like this for the last week or so."

Kacy's face went serious. He glared at Brianna like he could see right through her, first at her face, and then at her belly.

Brianna lifted her eyes towards Kacy, and noticed the knowing look on his face.

"What's that face for?" she snapped.

"You're not thinking what I'm thinking?"

"If you're thinking what I think you're thinking... then hell no I ain't thinking it!"

Brianna got back in the car without saying another word, but her mind was racing.

Kacy laughed, "Don't get mad at me. I got enough baby mama's to know the signs." He said. "We can stop by the pharmacy if you need to."

Brianna darted her eyes at him and said, "It's not even funny Kacy."

"Aiight… but you gone have to go eventually."

"Just take me home."

Brianna was speechless during the drive home. Her mind couldn't help but think about the times she'd had sex with Hakeem. She also thought about all the things she'd ever learned in sex ed. Birth control was only between 95 to 99 percent effective. Condoms were only 98. The only thing that was 100 percent was abstinence and she was way past that. Hakeem had always used a condom but she'd stop taking the pill when Tre died. And there was one time the condom broke. She shook her head and her body melted into the seat. Damn, she thought.

When Kacy pulled up to her condo, Brianna couldn't get out of the car quick enough. She darted into the lobby and towards the elevator. Even though it was the middle of the night, the lobby was well lit. The lights from the chandeliers reflected onto the marble floors. Light blue textured wallpaper dressed the walls, accented by elaborate crown molding and baseboards. Simple black and white landscape prints hung spaced on the walls. Eugene, the concierge, was posted at his desk off to the right of the elevator doors. Brianna had gotten in a habit of stopping by from time to time to chit chat with him. Not only had it been a good way to get priority treatment for packages and errands, it'd also paid off because Eugene made sure to keep an extra eye out for her. He wasn't a security guard by any means. But for special tenants like Brianna, he liked to think that he could protect her. If it was any other night, Brianna would have taken out a few minutes for him, but that night she just wasn't in the mood.

"Miss. Campbell," the concierge called out to her just as she passed him.

She stopped in her tracks and turned to him, "Hey Eugene. Can this wait till tomorrow?"

"Uhhh sure," he stammered, "but the message says urgent."

Brianna walked over to the desk and put her hand out for the note, "Who's it from?"

"The lady didn't leave her name, but she was short and dark

skinned girl with blonde hair."

"Really?" Brianna said with a grimace, "that bitch." She whispered to herself.

"Excuse me?"

"Nothing Eugene."

"Well, she was driving a hot car... ahhh I think it was a sliver-ish Maserati to be exact!"

"Thanks for the details," Brianna said with a quick wink and smile.

He placed the note in her hand and she rushed to the elevator.

When Brianna walked into her condo she yelled out, "Chhhhhhharrrrissssseeee!"

From the front door she could see all the way down the hallway to her sister's bedroom door. The mahogany hardwood floors were shiny and smooth. Brianna took of her heels and headed down the hall with bare feet.

Within seconds, Charrise popped her head out of the bedroom door.

"What the fuck you calling me like you my momma for?"

Brianna continued down the hallway towards her sister, "First, it's time to move."

"Huh?" Charisse asked.

"Second," Brianna took a deep breath, "I might be pregnant."

"Huh?" Charisse said for a second time with wide eyes looking down at her sister's belly.

Brianna lifted Charrise's face and looked her in the eyes. She opened her mouth, then closed it. Opened it again, and closed it once more.

"Pregnant? Really?"

Tears started to well up in Brianna's eyes. She shook her head and placed her hand on her temple as the tears started to plummet from her eyes.

Charrise took her sister by the hand and led her into the master suite. Brianna's bedroom was decorated in black and white with pops of purple. The high ceilings made room appear large and spacious. Sitting across from the floor to ceiling windows was her king sized bed dawned in black and white damask duvet. There were more pillows than she could count. The bed hugged her as laid on it after taking off her shoes and jacket. It wasn't the type of hug she wanted. Nothing like having her dead boyfriend, Tre's arms around her, but it would have to do.

"I'll be right back," Charrise said. "Don't move."

Thirty minutes later Charrise reappeared in the room with a bag in hand.

She poured out five different brands of pregnancy test on the bed. E.P.T., Clear Blue, First Response, Answer Plus and Advance.

"Really?" Brianna muttered. "I think one would have been enough."

"Well, I didn't have time to research the most accurate brand... so this was the next best option."

"I don't even think I have enough pee in me for all of those."

Charrise pulled out a big bottle of water from the bag.

"You just thought of everything didn't you?"

"Yup!" Charrise said pulling out the rest of the items from the bag. A box of Kleenex, candy bars, a jar of pickles, prenatal vitamins, and more.

Brianna opened the bottle of water and gulped it like the neighborhood wino downs a 40oz. Charrise opened all of the pregnancy test boxes and organized them with the test and instructions across the dresser.

"Which one you wanna try first?"

"It don't matter," Brianna said while she walked to the bathroom, "Just bring'em all."

Charisse did as she was told and handed them each to her sister as the stream of pee continued to provide samples for each indicator.

"You better be glad I love you!" she said as she lined each test up next to its coordinating instruction sheet.

Brianna emerged from the bathroom and began to dig into her Marc Jacobs purse. She pulled out the letter and opened it for the first time.

"What's that?" Charrise asked.

"This," Brianna said while dangling the letter in the air, "It's the reason we have to move. Let's read it while we wait for these results."

Brianna opened the envelop, and read it aloud.

Hey Bitch, I heard you went through the hood and tried to collect on something that don't belong to you. Should have already known you would, because you like fucking with other people shit! You would think you would have learned your lesson by now. But we know a hoe will be a hoe. I guess now you see who Hakeem really loves. By the way I hope you like the way my pussy tasted. Hakeem told me all he had you doing was sucking his dick! I guess that's all you good for slut. But let a real bitch let you know to stay away from my man shit. Or the next time I come to your house, I will bring my crew and you and your sister will get them asses whooped!

The sisters' eyes met.

"Who does that bitch think she is?" Charisse asked. "Uh un, I don' think we should be moving cause this chic talkin' shit."

"It's more than that. Too much shit has gone down here. And I def don't need that broad to know where I'm layin my head. It's time to move on and start fresh." Brianna tried to explain knowing that her sister was still too young and too naive to understand how things actually worked. Brianna was still trying to learn the ropes herself, but this seemed like an obvious decision to her. She didn't want to bring any unnecessary attention to herself... and the shit with Tiff was starting to get out of hand. As far as Brianna was concerned, it was better to be proactive rather than to be forced to be reactive.

Charisse shrugged and her eyes went over to the pregnancy tests that were waiting to tell a story, "We might need some space for a nursery any way."

Brianna rolled her eyes, "That's not even funny! Just go on and tell me the verdict."

Charisse went over to the dresser and took her time to carefully review the indicators and instructions of each test. She turned around with a plastered smile on her face, "I'm going to be an auntie."

Brianna threw her body back into the bed. She kicked and twitched on the bed like a two year old that wasn't getting her way. "Nooooooooooo!" she screamed, "This CANNOT be happening to me!"

Her sister leaned on the dresser and folded her arms across her chest. When Brianna finally quieted down Charisse said matter-of-factly. "You do know you have options, right?"

"What? Abortion?" Brianna said as if the thought disgusted her. Brianna always agreed that it was a woman's right to make that decision for herself. But she'd never considered having to abort a child of her own.

"That's the first obvious choice! I mean you can't be that far along. And I know you don't wanna have this baby."

Brianna looked up towards the ceiling and thought about it for a moment, "Dammit," she said. "Is my life ever just gonna be simple? I--- I---- I can't make that decision right now."

As Brianna sat there, she couldn't help but think about how her mother had been in a similar situation, pregnant by the wrong man. "What if she had decided to take the easy way out" Brianna said to herself. "My black ass wouldn't be here." She leaned back on the bed knowing although the circumstances were not what she hoped for; she couldn't make a rash decision.

Charrise shook her head, "You can't keep this baby Brianna."

She waived her off, "Stop talking to me right now Charrise. You're in no position to tell me what I can and can't do."

"Maybe not. But we both know you don't have a lot of time to make a decision. Think about it. If you keep this baby, you're gonna have to change your whole life. No more of this hustling fast paced life. No more of this quick money. You ready for that?"

"I already told you I need to process this. Shit, maybe having a normal life wouldn't be so bad." Brianna let her mind wander into a fantasy land where she was a proud mother raising a daughter. She thought about how she would give her child all the love that she'd never really received from her own mother. The idea of having a person that would lover her unconditionally, like Tre did, was inspiring. But she knew there was still something she could not offer the baby growing in her belly. It was the same thing her own mother could never offer her. A real father. The thought of finding a new man that was up to the task seemed impossible. Brianna wasn't sure that she could ever achieve normal status. She'd seen and done too much already.

Charrise sucked her teeth, "I had one already… this one's much better. Don't just think about yourself, sis. I need this too. And that baby… what if he or she comes out looking just like Hakeem. Then what yo ass gone do? You don't want to be staring at that for the rest of your life."

"Oooookayyyy Charrise! You've made your point, damn!"

"Aiight, I'll leave you alone. But think about what I'm sayin Bri."

Chapter 2

"Trapping Aint Dead"

"Last call for Boarding of flight 264 set for Charlotte, NC." Selena ran up to the gate just as the flight attendant was shutting the run way door. She quickly gave the older white female her ticket and was escorted to first class. Once in her seat Selena took a deep Breath and realized she had forgot to grab her ipod. "Damn she taught to herself, now I got to sit here and watch these bull shit as movies. I'm glad it's only a two hour flight!" Although Selena would never have admitted it, she was glad to be getting away from the city for a while. Things had gotten so hectic on the south-side of Queens. She had only been out of New York three times in her life. And that was only to visit her brothers in prison.

She was the true definition of a hood chick, although her appearance seemed to suggest otherwise. Her hair and complexion was the result of a Dominican father and a beautiful black mother with chocolate skin. She had taken on her father's complexion; a skin tone that most women thought was only available as a MAC foundation color and hair that they spent thousands of dollars on to have sown in. Her mother had passed down to her the type of body you would regularly see displayed in Major Hip Hop magazines. With a face that looked like it had not aged since she turned 16. The only blemish Selena had physically was a scar that ran from the right side of her mouth, back to her right ear lobe. Her skin had did all it could to mask the cut, but one would have to do a double take to make sure their eye's hadn't deceived them. Selena never wore makeup, she didn't need it. But she also didn't know how to put it on. Her mother had died when she was only five from stomach cancer, so she was raised in a house full of men. Selena had a total of six brothers and she was in the middle which meant she could never have a boyfriend when she was in school. Neither her older or younger brothers were having it. By the time they started going off to jail her younger brothers had gotten old enough to block any man who had an interest in her.

No matter how beautiful Selena was, no guy in the neighborhood wanted to have to deal with the Johnson family. Her brothers had made a name for themselves on the streets of South Jamaica Queens. They were all robbers and stick up kids. Even though they had family connections to get drugs and sell them for themselves her old brother Tony always said, "Why go through all that, when all I have to do is take it and let the other guy do all the work!"

Although her brothers never let her date they were always switching women; which is how Selena honed her fighting skills. She constantly had to put some bitch in check from spazing out on one of them. Her father had been a boxing champion back in the early 80's and still had all the equipment in the basement of their home. He would have the whole clan down stairs sparring with one another and Selena wasn't excluded. He knew where he had built a home for his family and they would definitely have to know how to fight! Their house sat about two blocks from the 40 project housing development. The neighborhood was bad then and had gotten worse over the years. The young niggas had picked up the gang bang from the west coast and it was getting crazier day by day. So when Selena received the call from her cousin Kacy, asking her to come down to Charlotte to help him out on some female shit. She was more than happy to oblige.

"Ma'am, ma'am please wake up." Selena woke up to the flight attendant nudging her. Much to her own surprise, she had slept the whole flight from New York to Charlotte. She got up and grabbed her bag from the overhead bin and began to exit the plane. Once she made it to the baggage claim she saw her cousin Kacy who she hadn't seen in a couple years but he still looked exactly the same.

"Wuz up cuz?" she said in her deep New York accent.

"Wuz good cuzzo!" Kacy said back to her as he grabbed her into an embrace. Let's grab your bags so we can get up outta here and I can give you the 411".

As Kacy and Selena headed towards downtown Charlotte to check into Salinas new home, the Westin Hotel, he began to give her details on the project he had thought she was perfect for. He told her that he was now the top security for a young female trapstar named Brianna and that he needed Selena to act like Brianna was the sister she never had.

"Trust me cuz, I been rocking with her for about four months and she definitely takes care of those who take care of her!"

It didn't take long for Selena to see that Kacy was telling the truth about Brianna. She had booked a Presidential Suite on the 25th floor of the hotel. This, Selena figured, was a great way to get a good look at her new stomping grounds. It was like her own studio apartment. Her first order of business was to strip down and get into the shower. That was until she walked in the bathroom and saw that there was a Jacuzzi tub. After growing up in a house full of testosterone, she could barely remember the last time she had been able to soak in a tub. She filled the tub with steamy hot water and immersed her body in the tub and started the jets.

Brianna and Charrise had toured condos all across the city. They'd looked downtown, in Ballantyne, NoDa, Huntersville, Dillworth, and Lake Norman. But nothing met Brianna's picky standards. Living in a condo, no matter how luxurious it was, just could not compare to the space and living style of a single family home. She missed having a yard and having neighbors that she didn't have to come into close contact with on a daily basis. She hated having to have forced casual conversation on the elevators, and answering questions about her life with lies to complete strangers that assumed friendship simply because they lived on the same floor. But she had grown accustomed to the added layer of security condo living had supplied her with. Tre had been dead for over a year yet she still woke up a few times a week in cold sweats from the nightmares that haunted her sleep. So no matter how much she wanted to live in a house, she just couldn't do it.

After a month of searching and whining from Charrise,

Brianna finally agreed on a compromise; a townhome in a gated community. As far as Brianna was concerned this was the best of both worlds. She was sold on the townhome when she found out that the community had a 24 hour security guard that would verify all guests prior to gaining access beyond the gate. It was icing on the cake when she learned of all features. The kitchen was stunning with cherry wood cabinets and oversized fridge, granite countertops and upgraded appliances. The plank hardwood floors sparkled like they had been freshly glossed and glistened as the sun shined through the tall windows. Brianna fell in love with the first floor master suite, and there was even a suite almost as large on the second floor with a balcony that Charrise quickly claimed. To top that, there was an office on the first floor that, and the two extra rooms joined by a jack and jill bathroom. Briana thought that one room could serve as a potential nursery and the other a guest room.

On move in day, Brianna stood at the end of her drive way directing movers as the lifted and carried in boxes and furniture. Her large Gucci shades shielded her eyes from the sun as she glared down the street to either side. She smiled at the freshly manicured lawns and peaceful breezed that cooled her on the humid summer day. When a shadow engulfed her, she automatically assumed that one of the movers had a question.

"You guys work fast, it looks like we're about done here." She turned around to face an unfamiliar smile. A smile that captivated her at first glance.

"Hello!" he started with a deep baritone voice, "My name is Brandon, I noticed that you are moving in and I just wanted to come by and welcome you to the community." He said with proper enunciation and grammar.

In that moment Brianna was grateful that she'd worn her shades realizing that they not only blocked the sun, but that they were also doing a pretty good job of hiding the fact that she was damn near molesting the guy with her eyes. Brandon wore a fitted heather gray Henley tee shirt, with blue jeans and slide-ins Nike. She couldn't believe that a man could looks so good without even trying, and could hardly imagine what he'd look like if he'd put a little effort in. She could see the bulge of his muscles and the pattern of this abs through his thin shirt.

She reached her hand towards him and coyly tilted her head to one side, "Hi, I'm Brianna. Thanks for the welcome."

She resisted the urge to allow the handshake to linger and instinctively removed her hand from his placing it on her still flat belly. Brianna reeled in her flirtatious behavior quickly remembering that she still had a huge decision to make. And aside from that, even as handsome as he was, she knew that her heart wasn't ready to start anything new.

"You'll like it here," he said. "Most people pretty much mind their business… but I couldn't help coming by when I noticed someone with a similar complexion moving in."

Brianna looked down at her caramel colored arm, and then into his amber colored face and laughed. "I understand. It was nice meeting you," she blurted out before he could say anything else.

"Ok," he said with a somber look on his face.

She went into the house quickly stood at the front window watching him walk away. Dayum! She said to herself.

"Kacy just called," Charrise said interrupting Brianna's thoughts.

"Ok, what'd he say?"

"That he's bringing his cousin Selena by to meet us."

"Now?" Brianna said with an attitude.

Charrise furrowed her eyebrows and replied, "Yes now! Why not now?"

"Cause we're in the middle of moving in! It's a mess in here. Uh un… I'm calling him back right now. I'm hungry anyway so we can meet them out for dinner. Plus, I need the meet this chick first before I let her all up in our space."

Charrise shook her head and rolled her eyes, "You know what?"

"No, what?"

"I'll be glad when you figure out what you're going to do about this seed cause I can't take much more of your mood swings and attitudes about nothing."

"Whatever bitch!" She laughed, "I ain't that bad!"

She looked Brianna up and down and shook her head disapprovingly. "Let's just get out of here… food seems to help. Let's feed this little monster you have growing inside you and maybe you'll be back to normal, at least for a little while."

Brianna changed into a flowing blue maxi dress with platform wedge sandals. She pulled her cinnamon brown hair back into a lose ponytail and snapped in platinum hooped earrings. Brianna added bangles to her right wrist and a necklace with a diamond pendant of the letter T. For her finishing touches she added dark pink gloss and touched up her mascara. "Ready," she yelled to Charrise upstairs.

Charrise came down stairs in fitted grey skinny jeans and a dark purple tunic that hung lazily off of her left shoulder. She wore her hair bone straight with a part on the side. Her long mane cascaded over her shoulders and down to her back. They looked around at their new home. Charrise had painstakingly directed the movers to place the furniture exactly the way she wanted it, but the boxes had been scattered about the rooms. The two bobbed and weaved along the rows of boxes towards the doors. Out of nowhere Charisse came to a stop with Brianna right on her heels.

"What the fuck?" Brianna screeched.

Charrised turned around abruptly, "Well..." she started, "I was going to wait for you to tell me, but since you haven't opened your mouth up about it yet, I figure I might as well get it out there."

"Tell you what?"

"Tell me about that man."

"What man?"Brianna asked incredulously.

Charrise crooked her head from left to right, "Don't try to act all confused."

Brianna flailed her hands wildly, "But I am confused."

"Who was that guy you were outside talking to earlier." She asked directly.

"Oh," Brianna puffed out loudly, "Just a neighbor!"

"Ummm hummmm," she moaned suspiciously.

"Don't start... you know I'm not even on the market right now." She said patting her tummy, "and besides, he's not even my type."

"Whatever chick... you keep telling yourself that lie." Charrise commented with a laugh.

Brianna and Charrise met Kacy and Selena at the Cheesecake Factory. Brianna had been having a craving for cheesecake that she just couldn't shake. The restaurant was crowded as usual, but

Brianna and Charrise had made it there just before the rush and had been seated in a booth that was tucked away in the back of the restaurant. When she saw Kacy walking through the crowd, at first she couldn't tell which woman was with him. To the right of him was a dark brown woman with short curly hair, she had a square face that made her look masculine but large brown eyes that softened her appearance. Brianna thought to herself that this girl would be fit for the job. But when she looked again she noticed a woman with a young face and silky jet black hair that bobbed at her chin. Her face was beautiful and striking and a bit familiar. As Kacy continued to walk through the crowd it became obvious to Brianna that the familiar look of the gorgeous girl was because of the family resemblance she had with Kacy. This girl was not at all what she had imagined her bodyguard would look like, and Kacy had some explaining to do.

It wasn't until the pair was escorted right up to the table that Brianna noticed the long scar that went up the side of Selena's face. She was immediately curious to find out the story behind the wound. Just as Kacy started to introduce Selena a waiter arrived with appetizers.

"Damn," he exclaimed, "Y'all couldn't at least wait till we got here to order!"

Charrise cut her eyes over towards Brianna, "You know greedy over here just couldn't stand to wait."

Kacy gave Brianna a knowing look, and sat down. The waiter began placing an array of appetizers in the center of the table. Hot spinach dip, roadside sliders, fried mac and cheese, crab wontons and tex mex eggrolls.

"Well at least I tried to order a little something to please everyone."

Kacy and Selena sat down at the table and everyone loaded their plates with their own combinations of starters and dug in. Between bites, Brianna attempted to perform a conversational interview with Selena.

"So Selena," she began, "Kacy's been my right hand man, but I guess I've been taking up too much of his time because he insisted that we get you down to here to fill in the gaps. You think you're up to the task?"

Selena wasted no time in listing her credentials. "No doubt," she said with a thick but sultry New York accent, "I've been through a lot back in NY, and let me tell you I always come out on top."

Brianna was impressed, "Well I don't know how much Kacy has told you about me, but I've just come off of a real tough year... and really I just want you to know that I appreciate you coming down here to help me out. I think we'll make good friends, but more importantly I think we'll do great business together."

Selena smiled, "I agree."

"We just moved, but once we get settled in, I'd love for you to stop by and spend some time with me and my sister. How are things at the Westin?"

Selena's mind wandered back to the Jacuzzi tub, "They're wonderful," she smiled.

"Great!"

The waiter reappeared to take their orders. One by one they each told their choices to him as he jotted down on his pad in a hurried pace.

Before they knew it the table was overflowing with steaming hot food. They all dug in and silence engulfed the table as everyone devoured their meals.

Chapter 3

Charrise and Selena blended in with ease as they headed south on Interstate-85 south. The four-door Toyota Camry attracted little, if any, attention at all. All the nervous energy Charisse had when she first started making these drives nearly a year before had completely vanished. Those days she stayed either in the middle or far right lane, managing to go no more than five miles over the speed limit. It didn't take long, before she realized that driving that slow wasn't doing anyone any favors. She bobbed and weaved through the other cars with little effort. She could do this drive in her sleep. Selena sat in the passenger seat looking out of the window as they drove through one small town after another.

"You miss your family yet?" Charrise asked breaking the silence of the ride.

"Ummmm," Selena thought before answering, "Yes and no. I mean, I miss them, but it's nice to be away. Even nicer not to be surrounded by men all day," she said with a laugh.

"Oh yeah, that's right. You didn't have any sisters."

"Nope, just me and the boys."

Charrise shook her head, "I don't know what I would have done without my sister… even better I don't know what she woulda done without me!"

"That's the way I feel about my brothers. But there are just some things boys will never understand about women. And don't even get me started on them being over protective!"

"I bet!"

"They wouldn't let any guys get within a 50 mile radius of me."

"Don't tell me you've never had a boyfriend."

"Not a real one… but let's just say I had to learn to sneak. That wasn't easy either. It always seemed like the guys I liked we're my brother's friends. They were too scared of my brothers and dad to say anything to me. And I was too afraid that we'd get caught if they did."

"So what'd you do?"

Selena looked at her with eyes that asked, you won't tell anyone will you?

Charrise did a quick glance around her shoulder, "It's just you and me girl! I won't judge you!"

"Ok," Selena said, "My oldest brother had this one friend."

"Uh huh."

"It was his best friend, you know. He was like a part of our family." Selena paused.

"Go on…" Charrise urged.

"So he would be over to the house all the time. Would spend the night, everything. We were tight, and nobody really cared cause, like I said, he was like family. Anyway, one morning I was up early, before everybody… and he just happened to be up too. I think all the boys had gone out the night before and my dad was already at work. We were chillin' watching this movie, it was some Spike Lee movie… I don't remember which one. I just remember that it was a lot of sex in it. We were both at that age… hormones raging. Before I knew it, he was slipping his hand under my night gown, and I was letting him finger me. You know when your 15 and you ain't never had none, fingering is the best thing ever!"

Charisse laughed and nodded, "I remember those days."

"So you know what happened after that. It started with fingering and ended with fucking."

Charrise belted out a loud laugh, "how'd ya'll keep that quiet."

"It was hard, but he had as much too loose as I did so he never said anything. We just snuck around. I got so good at sneaking that I ended up catching that son of bitch with his real girlfriend!"

"Say what?" Charrise asked dramatically.

"Girl yeah! We were supposedly secret boyfriend/girlfriend

for like two years. All that time I thought it was a secret cause my brothers and dad would trip, but come to find out it was because I was never his real girl friend."

"What did you do when you found out?"

"Besides have a broken heart... I went after him... and that bitch."

"Damn!"

"That's how I got this scar on my face."

Charrise looked at Selena's scar as if she hadn't noticed it before. But she had. Both she and Brianna had discussed the scar and the possible situations that would have yielded that type of mark on someone's face.

"Usually when I had a beef with someone I could tell my brothers. They'd always make me fight my own battles, but they also always had my back just in case I couldn't beat someone solo. But in this case I couldn't tell them."

"Right... right."

"I ended up following them for a whole day. Watching him do things with her that he could never do with me. Taking her out to eat, shopping, to the movies. That mutha fucker had never even bought me a damn thing. Said that he didn't want nobody asking me where I'd got it from. By the end of the night, I was furious. I mean... the level of rage in me... I'd never felt so mad and hurt at the same time before. I ended up charging at them in the darkness. It was an ambush... like something in the movies, or at least that's the way I remember it," Selena chuckled, "I don't think he even realized who I was when he pulled out a knife. He was just trying to protect himself. Cut me right down the side of my face. Blood was everywhere."

"Damn."

"They started to run when I fell down, but I called out to him. He must have recognized my voice because he ran back to me. Told the bitch to keep going without him. She didn't even hesitate."

"What'd he say."

"Not a damn thing... he already knew what it was. He just took me home. He told my family that some girls jumped me. Of course I didn't dispute it. I just let him make up a story. When my brothers asked me more questions I wouldn't tell them anything. I told them to let it go. Eventually, they did."

Before Charrise had a chance to make any comments she realized that it was time to exit the highway to get off on Lenox Rd towards Lenox Square Mall. Even though Charrise knew exactly where she was going, she still didn't say anything about Selena's scar or what she'd just shared. She didn't really know what to say at first. When they made it to the first light she reached her arm around her and pulled her close.

"I'm sorry you had to go through that alone. But just so you know, you've got two sisters in me and Brianna. We might not be able to fight like your brothers, but we'll always have your back."

"Thank you," Selena whispered.

Charrise found a parking space outside of Neiman Marcus and headed inside with Selena beside her.

"So what's next?" Selena asked like a curious child.

"Next we make a quick key exchange, maybe do a little shopping, and then we head back home."

"That simple, huh?"

"Yup…" Charrise said as she stopped quickly to take a look at a pair of pink Jimmy Choo crocodile print sandals. Charrise made a mental note of their location and head out of the department store. She pulled her iPhone from her purse and checked her messages. Her new connect Monte would meet her in the food court. Monte wasn't as talkative or handsome as Andre had been, but that was just the way Charrise liked it. After her experience with Andre, she didn't want or need any reason for things to get messy again. These trips were strictly business… except of course for the great shopping; her only non-business luxury she allowed herself. She'd convinced herself that shopping made the trips seem believable, just in case anyone was following her. She knew that the odds of that were slim, but she would take any excuse to make a few fashionable purchases.

In the food court, Charrise spotted Monte standing in the Chic-fil-a line. Even though she didn't know much about him, it was obvious that he was a sucker for a chicken sandwich and waffle fries. It never failed, every time she met him he was either in line, or on his way out of the line. Monte found himself a booth in the middle of the food court, and Charrise followed his lead. When the two women approached the table Monte looked up quickly. He eye balled Selena for a moment before inviting the pair to take a seat.

"You not eating today?" He asked in a deep baritone voice.

"I'm good," Charrise responded, "You hungry Selena."

"Yeah a little."

"Ok, go ahead and grab something."

As soon as Selena walked away, Monte asked, "Who's the new girl?"

"Security."

"What the fuck you need security for with me?" he asked getting defensive.

She rolled her eyes, "Not for you! For home. But today, I'm showing her the ropes."

"Oh aiight," he responded offering her the fries with the key cupped in his hand.

"I don't mind if I do," Charrise said as she grabbed a waffle fry and a key out of his carton replacing it with a key of her own.

As Selena was making her way back to the table, Monte was exiting.

"It was nice to meet you…" he hesitated.

"Selena," she told him with a smile.

Monte nodded and headed towards the mall exit.

"That was quick," Selena said sitting back down with a salad.

"We're professionals," Charrise smiled. "Quick and efficient."

Brianna smoothed out the piece of hair she'd coiled around her finger, and walked slowly over towards nurse. She was a short white lady with auburn hair cut into a sleek bob. She had a wide smile with straight white teeth.

"Hello Ms. Campbell, my name is Amy." She smiled and led Brianna beyond the double doors of the doctor's office. "How are you doing today?"

Brianna smiled politely attempting to conceal her nervous energy. Her eyes darted down the long hall. The walls were adorned with pictures of pregnant women and babies in a matte finish inside silver frames. They complimented the light lavender paint perfectly.

The nurse led Brianna to a bathroom, "We'll need to collect a sample from you. Use on of the containers on the shelf, write your name on it and place it in that door." She pointed to a small metal door on the wall. "When you're finished meet me in room two. The doctor will be in to see you shortly."

Alone in the restroom, Brianna frowned. She despised public restrooms, and although this one was much nicer than average, she still hated the thought of pissing where strangers had done the same thing or more. She squatted over the toilet, careful not to let her skin come in contact with the seat. She hovered there and steadied her hand in the proper position allowing a steady stream to fill the cup.

This is it, she thought to herself. Today would be the day she'd find out for sure if she was pregnant. Even though all the signs were there, a part of her wouldn't believe it until it was made official by a professional. Brianna put the lid on the cup and closed it behind the metal door. She walked into the room that Amy had instructed her to and waited for the doctor.

"Ok, Brianna. It's good to see you." Dr. Abner said as he entered the room. He glanced down at his chart and asked, "Do you know the date of your last cycle."

"Honestly Doc, I really don't remember."

He smiled, "Welp, we'll need to do a quick ultra sound on you. That way we can…"

Brianna cut him off, "Ultra sound? So that means I'm really pregnant."

"Oh yeah, you're definitely pregnant," he laughed.

Brianna laid back on the examination table.

Dr. Abner explained, "An ultra sound will allow us to measure the fetus and give us a good idea of how far along you are."

Brianna was speechless. It was as if she was hearing this information all over for the first time. The confirmation of pregnancy weighed so heavy on her that she couldn't lift herself up to face the doctor or utter any words to validate that she'd heard anything he was saying. She heard the door open as Dr. Abner continued to speak, "Amy will take you down to the ultra sound tech and we'll go from there."

Brianna lay stone faced on the table with her shirt pulled up and a blanket covering everything below her waist. The Ultrasound technician squeezed a dollop of warm lubricating gel on her belly and used a probe to search for the baby.

On the screen Brianna could only make out a black pit surrounded by a gray static haze. Then she noticed the technician focusing in on the black pit. She turned the volume up on the ultrasound machine and out of the speakers Brianna could hear the rapid 'Ba-dum, ba-dum, ba-dum, ba-dum…'.

"Is that…"

The technician nodded she smiled, "That's your baby's heartbeat." She pointed toward the monitor, you see that?"

Brianna sat up on her elbow and stared at the monitor, "That peanut looking thing?"

"Yeah, that's your baby. But look closer. Do you see that little flicker?"

"Yes," Brianna said as a tear escaped her eye.

"That's the heart beating. It's strong and healthy. Now let me take a few measurements here for the doctor."

Brianna laid back onto the table and wiped away her tear. She quickly sucked in all of her emotions determined to hold herself together.

Back in the examination room, Dr. Abner entered the room and announced, "Looks like you're about eight weeks pregnant dear."

Everything he said after that was a complete blur to Brianna. She woke up in her bed and picked up her phone to check the time. It was 2:00 am the next morning. She couldn't believe she'd slept so long. She didn't remember leaving the doctor's office or driving home. Brianna looked down and realized that she was only wearing her panties and bra; she looked over to the floor and noticed her clothing tossed to the side. The first thing she could think go do was to go look in a mirror. She rushed into her bathroom and turned on the lights. Turning to her side she looked at the small round bulge that forming on her belly. It didn't quite look like a baby bump, rather just like she'd just finished eating a big meal. She turned another 90 degrees and looked over her shoulder. From the back her normal hour glass curves were still defined.

The sound of the baby's heartbeat rang loudly in Brianna's head. 'Ba-dum, ba-dum, ba-dum, ba-dum…'.

Chapter 4

"Herman make sure you turn those ribs before they burn!" Lorain shouted at her husband who was minding the grill.

"Rain who cooking this food? Me or you?" Herman screamed back. "You know I know what I'm doing on this grill. And I'm not letting nothing mess up my son's graduation day. He's only the second Campbell male to graduate high school!" he beamed with pride.

Jonathan had about forty friends and relatives over for his graduation cook out. Everyone in the neighborhood could smell the food and hear the loud music blasting Anytime someone entered the backyard Herman had to remind Jonathan to show them the watch he had giving him for graduation. It had taken him nearly four months to save up enough money to purchase the $1200 Movado watch. It was the perfect gift he thought to himself.

"Every man has to have a real time piece," he'd told his wife Lorain with a big smile when he revealed it to her the night before the graduation.

"Jon, show your Uncle Bobby your watch. He don't know nothing about no Movado! And Lorain put my Frankie Beverly & Maze on!" Herman exclaimed.

"Is this your party or Jon's?" Lorain asked with a laugh.

"That's what I was about to ask Uncle Bobby chimed in. And I hope you had enough money left over after that watch to buy something to sip on because you know I'm getting drunk for my nephew big day!"

"Ah nigga you will get drunk for any day!" Herman shouted back, "and you know I got something in the cooler, just make sure you leave me some!"

"Beep. Beep, Beep.."

"Who is that laying on that horn like they crazy in my drive way!" Herman shouted. "Jon go around there and see who that is and if that's one of your little friends ask them who told them to pull their car up in my yard!"

As Jonathan made his way around the side of the house he saw exactly who had a nerve to pull up on his father's lawn. It was his sister Charisse. She was hanging out the window of the car waving with one hand and using the other one to hit the horn. He looked down at the beautiful 2012 Dodge Charger. It was midnight black on black and was sitting on 22 inch chrome rims. He could hear the Hemi motor and off road exhaust system purring.

"Damn sis this your new ride? He asked as he approached the driver side door. Charisse was exiting the vehicle.

"Nope Charisse," answered back quickly. "It's for a very special man in our sister Brianna's life."

"Where is she anyway and who is this special man?"

"You know she wanted to be here but she had some business to take care of." Charisse wasn't sure if Jonathan knew about the ongoing feud between their father and half-sister. And she wasn't about to be the one who brought it up to him. "And the special man is you crazy!"

"Oh shit, are you serious?" Jonathan started running around screaming and then he jumped into the car. He immediately turned on the radio and could hear the Bose system blaring. "Damn," he thought. "I don't have to do anything, this car already has everything."

The music from the car began to drown out the sounds of Frankie Beverly coming from the small home stereo. And everyone began to make their way to the front of the house to see where all the new noise was coming from. Before Herman and Lorain could make their way from the side of the house, they could hear people coming back around shouting "His sister brought him a new car for graduation!" Herman immediately stopped walking and turned around to go back, but was stopped by his brother Bobby.

"Boy that's a hellva car your daughter brought that boy! Shit he riding better than you nigga. Let me see if I can get my nephew to run me to the store. Hell better yet give me Brianna's number let me see if she can help her Unk out with a couple of dollars!"

Herman looked at him with disgust "Nigga get out my face!"

Charisse made her way to the backyard and gave Jonathan some time to cruise in his new car. She opened her arms wide headed straight towards her mother. She wrapped her arms around Lorraine and felt the matching embrace.

"Hey Ma! I see ya'll sure do know how to throw a party. Look at all these people." She said looking at the nearly full back yard. "Where's dad at?"

"I don't know. He got missing when you came in the new car. It was real nice of Brianna to get that for him. She ain't coming?"

Charisse looked at Lorraine with a peaked eyebrow, "Now you know!"

"I know, I know. I just thought she might come to see her baby brother ya know."

Charrise shrugged, "I think it take a whole lot more to get her back over here."

She took another look around at all her family and old friends from the neighborhood. She didn't miss this life. She almost felt out of place wearing stilettos amongst flip flops. Everyone looked like there were in complete bliss dancing in the middle of the grassy lot and eating from a homemade buffet. Lorraine and Herman had gone through the trouble of renting a tent and tables for guest to have a comfortable place to sit and eat. Charrise had kept up with giving money to her mother each month to make ends meet in their household. It seemed like things were turning around for her parents.

"I still don't see dad," she said again cranking her neck from side to side searching the crowd.

"Well check in the house."

Charrise walked to the house and slide the sliding glass door open. Herman was sitting in his La-Z-Boy with a beer in his hand. The TV. wasn't on, so Charrise couldn't figure out why he was excluding himself from the party. Herman was typically the life of the party at these type of events. He took pride in his BBQ and being the hostess with the mostess. The man he presented outside of the home was completely different to the man that Charrise had sometimes watched terrorize her mother and sister. But she was his baby girl and could do no wrong. Charisse walked around the chair and noticed Herman staring ahead with a grimace on his face.

"Hey Daddy," she said. "What's up with the sour puss?"

Herman looked up at Charisse and without even the slightest hint of happiness to see his baby girl. Charisse couldn't believe it. In all her life her father had never missed an opportunity to gush over his darling baby girl.

"Daddy?" She said as she walked closer to him.

Herman stood up quickly and grabbed Charisse's arm. "Where tha hell your sister get that money to buy that car?" He snapped.

Charisse tried to pull away unsuccessfully. She saw a familiar look in his eyes. A look that he had always saved especially for Brianna. She yanked away forcefully, "That hurts daddy!" she shouted.

"Answer me!" he yelled.

"What do you mean where" she retorted, "Brianna works! I work!"

"Ummmm hummm," he said as he began to pace the floor. "I know ya'll are up to no good over there. Do you think I'm stupid!" he continued to yell at Charrise. "You done came up in here with all that name brand shit on. All that goddamn make up! I didn't raise you like that! You come up in here tryna make me look bad. Me! Let me tell you something little girl. I've been around and I know a lot more than you think I do. And if you think that I'm going to let this shit slide you got another thing coming."

Charrise looked down at the floor to avoid eye contact, "What slide daddy? I don't understand why you're so upset."

"All you need to know is that that little chump change you've been passing along to your mother every month ain't gone cut it no more. If you expect me to keep quiet I'ma need more."

Charisse started to panic. She could feel her heart racing. She'd never considered the fact that her family would start to question how much money she was making and how. She certainly hadn't expected to get blackmailed by her own father.

"How much more?" she stammered.

"At least double!" he shouted, "or else... Now get outta my house."

Herman turned his back to Charrise and continued to pace the floor.

In the kitchen, Lorriane hurried to sneak back out of the kitchen door. She'd overheard everything, but had learned a long time ago not to intervene when Herman was in a fit of rage. Right behind her Charrise came bursting through the door. Lorraine busied herself at the grill checking on the meat. She looked up and caught Charisse's eye.

"Is everything ok baby?"

Charrise walked over to her mother, kissed her on the cheek and said, "Yeah Mama, everything's good. I'm about to get outta here."

"What?" Lorraine pressed, "Why baby? You just got here." She didn't really know if she wanted to hear the truth or not. Either way, there was nothing she could really do about it.

"Ummmm," Charrise hesitated and shrugged, "Me and Brianna are gonna take him out tonight. I'll let ya'll celebrate now, but I'ma go rest up for tonight." She tried to form a smile on her face, but it looked more like she'd caught a foul odor in the summer breeze.

"Ok," Lorraine said a bit relieved. She gave Charrise another hug and walked her to the front of the house where Jonathan was riding back into the driveway.

"Where you goin' Sis," he said as he hopped out of the car.

"I'm going to rest up for tonight."

"Tonight? What's happening tonight?"

"It's you're day boo... We'll let mom and dad handle the cookout now, but tonight me and Brianna go t you! You better get ready to party like you've never partied before!"

"Bet! I can't wait!" Jonathan was smiling like a kid on Christmas morning.

"You know we got you... but only on one condition," Charrise hesitated.

"Whatever it is you got it!"

"Great... cause I'ma need a ride home real quick."

Chapter 5

"Bri are you ready yet, damn we just going shopping, can't you just throw something on already?" Charrise had met up with Brianna at Selena's new place. Once Brianna had spent a little one on one time with her, she knew that she'd keep Selena around for a while so a more permanent residence seemed more suitable.

"Charisse, give me a break, you just want to get down stairs to see if you can run into Cam again!" It had been two weeks since Brianna and Charisse had accidently found out that Cam Newton the star quarterback for the Carolina Panthers was living in the same building they'd moved Selena into. Even Brianna had to admit that she was taken aback by his beautiful smile and chiseled body. But once he started bouncing the basketball around her and Charisse in the elevator. She was reminded that he was only 19 years old.

"How are you ladies doing today?" Cam yelled over the noise of the bouncing ball.

"Maybe if you'd quit bounce that ball we could answer!" Brianna yelled back.

"What you say?"

"I said quit bouncing that damn ball!" Brianna shouted it louder.

"My fault, I didn't mean to make your curse," Cam said with a big smile. Before she could say something back, Charisse jumped in.

"Cam don't pay her no attention, she not a morning person, I would love to take you one-on-one sometime." Brianna shot Charisse a 'you going that hard' look.

Charisse kept going, "By the way, you my favorite football player and I'm your biggest fan."

"Well thank you Ms?"

"My name is Charisse and this meanie is my sister Brianna, but everyone calls her Bri." again Brianna looked at Charisse telling her with her eyes 'don't be given out my info!'

"Well it's nice to meet both of you and since you're my biggest fan, I'm going to make sure I get you some tickets to my next game!"

Ever since that day Charisse had spent plenty of time hanging with Selena trying to run back into him so she could take him up on that offer.

"Look Bri, I ain't looking for nobody, but if I run back into him I'm going hard this time!"

"Shit! You don't think you were going hard last time bitch?" Brianna said with a laugh. Bri's laugh made Charisse start to chuckle.

"Forget you! I ain't like you. You act like you allergic to dick all of a sudden. That damn magic bullet going to hurt you one day!" both girls busted out with even greater laughter.

As they began to approach the elevator, Brianne remembered that she forgot to leave Selena a note letting her know that they were going to the mall. At some point every day, Selena would go for a 5k run and she'd left right before Charrise came in. Brianna knew Selena wouldn't get back for at least 30 minutes and wouldn't want to go to the mall, especially not with them. Brianna and Charisse where both mall rats who could spend a whole day shopping. On the other hand, Selena hated shopping. She preferred to go in the store, pick an outfit off one of the mannequins and be out. Since Brianna knew how she was, she figured she would just find Selena something to wear for that night. They had booked VIP at club Lux off South Blvd. The club had already scheduled Rick Ross and Brianna knew he was Jonathan's favorite artist so he figured that would be the perfect way to celebrate with him since she'd promised herself a long time ago that she'd never step foot in the home she'd grown up in again.

She and Charisse always made sure that their baby brother had the latest gear and shoes to match. Brianna loved showering him with gifts, she figured that he was the one man left in her life that she could show love to and not worry about it coming back to bite her in the ass. Besides, Jonathan was the perfect kid. He stayed on the Honor Role and had already got accepted to Clark University in Atlanta for pre-med.

Brianna grabbed the note pad and scribbled Selena a quick note. She posted the sticky paper against the refrigerator. She knew Selena would be coming in from running to get her specially made energy shake, so she couldn't miss it. When she arrived back at the elevator, Charisse was holding the door open button.

"About time you got back, my finger about to fall off, what were you doing writing her a love letter?"

"Don't you be trying me like that! But I be seeing the way you be watching them girls when we at Onxy." Brianna shot back with a smirk.

"No sis, I'm strictly dickly. Speaking of dick let's get down stairs and she if my baby daddy is in the lobby!"

When they arrived at the lobby, Charisse was disappointed to see no Cam, but the concierge greeted them quickly. They were there so much that he knew them by name.

"Good morning Ms. Campbell's, I have already sent for your vehicle, it will be just a minute."

"Thanks Charles, Brianna reached in her purse and grabbed a twenty dollar bill and placed it into his hand. When the car pulled up Brianna and Charisse got inside and headed towards South Park Mall. As they road down Sharon rd. Brianna carefully observed the white women out with their children walking down the perfectly manicured lawns. She couldn't help but to think what her life would have been like if she grew up in the same environment. Or, if Tre was still alive. 'Well,' she thought to herself as she checked her reflection in the rear view mirror, 'you've got to play with the cards you dealt!' Besides her life wasn't all that bad, at least she didn't have to get up every day and go to work for pennies; or even worse have to fuck some sorry ass nigga for a few dollars to make ends meet.

"Charisse plug in my iPod and find my song… oh, and make sure the volume is up!" Charisse scrolled through the iPod until she found the new Mary J song entitled Mr. Do Wrong. Almost immediately the lyrics and Drake's voice came blasting through the speakers.

"Don't it seem like, like I'm always there when it matters

But missing most of the other time, a terrible pattern
The rewards I see from working made me an addict
There's way more people that want it than people that have it"

Both girls snuggled back into soft leather seats of the new Range Rover sport, enjoying the sounds of the premier sound system. Once they arrived at the entrance of the mall. Brianna pulled up to the Valet service. The valets grabbed both doors and reached her the Valet ticket. The girls exited and headed into the mall.

"Mental note Charisse, we will be stopping at the Cheesecake Factory, so I can get a slice of that chocolate mousse cake."

"Aight! You know them hips spreading, your ass will be out there running with Selena in a minute!" they both laughed at the comment.

Brianna rubbed her belly, "Well I can get away with it for now."

Charisse rolled her eyes and kept walking without a word.

"Ok, our first two stops are BCBG and Micheal Kors we got to find Selena something hot for tonight. If you think it's been a minute for me having some dick, you don't want to know the last time she was touched!"

After finding outfits for Charisse and Selena in Michael Kors they made their next stop. In BCBG, Brianna tried on a Persian blue dress with dolman sleeves that hugged tightly on her but and hits, but hung loosely around her waist. She walked out of the dressing room and did a slow spin for Charisse's to view.

"What'chu think about this?"

"Ummm," Charisse hesitated, "it's cute but... that's not really your style."

"Well I have to do something to hide this growing baby hump."

"I know exactly what you can do!" Charisse announced.

"That's really easy for you to say. You didn't hear the kid's heart beat!"

"What?" Charisse sat there wide eyed. "When did you hear that?"

"The day before yesterday when I went to the OB."

"Damn sis, that's heavy."

"I know right! Shit! I can't get that sound outta my head. It's like…. Like…"

Charisse shook her head and looked down, "Like you're making a person… creating a life."

Brianna nodded, "Exactly. I don't know if I can go through with an abortion after hearing that."

"I feel you. I know I've given you my opinion, but honestly, you know I'll support you either way right?" Charrise stood up and hugged her sister.

"I know sissy," Brianna said with a small smile.

"Look, while we're having this little warm and fuzzy moment, I've got something I need to tell you."

"Oh lord," Brianna placed her hand on her temple, "I hate when you start a conversation with that!"

"Yep… and you should, cause this ain't good."

Charrise pushed Brianna back into the dressing room and entered in with her. She lowered her voice almost to a whisper and explained what had gone down at the graduation cookout with her dad.

Brianna was furious. "I don't need this shit from him! Like I don't already have enough on my plate!" She redressed into her clothes and stormed out of the dressing room with Charrise right on her tail. When she whipped around the corner the Sales Associate was ready with complementary accessories.

"Thanks Janet," Brianna said correcting her bad mood quickly.

Janet winked at her, "You know I know what you like."

Brianna took a glance at the things and had to admit that Janet definitely knew her taste well. She swiftly pulled out a wad of cash and followed Janet to the register.

As the pair walked to pick up their car from the valet, Brianna's mind was burning with hate. It was like her step-father would never stop terrorizing her. She'd thought that after she'd left home she would never have to worry about him ever again, and had never expected that giving her sister a job would eventually land them in this type of situation. Sure, she'd always known that Herman was grimy to his core, but Brianna didn't think he had it in him to put his own flesh and blood in harm's way.

In the car Charrise said, "So what should we do? Give him the money to keep him quiet?"

Brianna just shook her head, "Fuck him! This is exactly why I never wanted you to be giving them money in the first place," she yelled. "That muthafucka has always hated me... so much so that he's even willing to bring you down to get to me!"

Charrise was practically speechless. It had stung her to her core to see the level of animosity her father had in his eyes when he was threatening her. She had always despised the way Herman mistreated Brianna, but through the years she kept her love for her father separate from the love of her sister. Some way she'd been able respect him as her own father and hate him as the evil stepfather of Brianna.

"And the sad part is Charrise... I've never done anything to deserve this."

"You're right Bri," Charrise tried to reassure her, "I shouldn't have even said anything. I'll take care of it. Just forget I even mentioned it."

"Oh hell no! I'll never forget this shit. I got something for his ass... but right now... today... we're celebrating for Jonathan and we're NOT going to let him get in the way!"

That night Brianna decided to take out the new truck she had just purchased a few weeks prior. She didn't know what it was, this new fascination she was having with SUV's, especially with the cost of gas. But when she saw the 2012 Lexus truck in pearl black with cocaine white interior she had to have it. Maybe it was the thought of the new family edition she was carrying in her womb.

"We ready" Charrise yelled interrupting Brianna's private moment.

"Yea we really ready, this time" Selena add looking at Charrise, because she was the one they was waiting on. Once the girls reached downtown Charlotte, it was evident that the club was pack. Traffic was at a standstill for what look like 2 miles.

"Bri, make a left and see what it look like on the South Blvd side" Charrise suggested.

Brianna took her advice and made the left, when she arrived at South Blvd, the traffic was worst then Tryon St.

"Thanks a lot lil sis, this shit is worse, I knew I should have made your back seat driving ass, drive for real!"

"Fuck that, you get your pretty ass on out and I'll whip this big bitch believe that!" All the girls laughed at once.

"And you better quit all that cursing too, you know your nephew can hear you and what's he going to think of his potty mouth auntie?"

"Shit, the same thing he going to think of his potty mouth momma, when she gets mad!" They all laughed again.

It took about 45 minutes before the girls finally made it into a parking space and out of the truck. But only took seconds before the men began blowing the horns and hollering out the windows. Selena's dress had her body on full display. Her breast and her ass look so full in the dress that one would wonder how she got it on. Brianna, although trying to conceal her current condition, look like she was on her way to a New York runway. Her hair was flowing half way down her back and her face looked stunning. Charrise was bringing up the rear and was definitely enjoying the attention. She knew when she picked out her dress, that with her slim frame and size 36 double d breasts, that the opening in the middle of her chest would keep the men's eyes stuck on her. She also knew that although her ass was not as round as Brianna or Selena's, no one would know with the right dress and stilettos. She had also perfected the "my body is banging" walk that made it sound like the Budweiser horse's where nearby. Once they made it into the club and into their VIP section, The bottles began coming one after another.

"Jonathan better hurry up and get here, because his sister is about to be fucked all the way up!" Charrise yelled over the blurring music.

Someone in the booth beside them had taken it upon themselves to light up some serious loud weed. The smell and smoke forced their way into Brianna's face. Selena could see that Brianna was fighting back the disturbing smell, but it wasn't working very good. She leaned out the booth and looked over at one of the guys who was tooting on the blunt. Selena in a very seductive manner motioned with her finger to come closer. The man did as he was told and got up and headed her way.

"What it do shawtey, you trying to blow with a Nigga tonight?" he asked in a deep southern draw.

"No I'm good babe, I was just hoping you could tame the smoke down, because my friend is a little under the weather and the smoke is really getting to her. Plus I don't want it all in my clothes," she asked in her little girl voice.

"No problem beautiful, and If I got some in that outfit, please let me take it off and buy you another one."

Selena smiled, "Maybe you can just start with a drink and we can see how that goes."

"Fair enough, what you drinking on?

"Cirroc and pineapple juice."

"I got you, I'll be right back." the guy ran off trying to find a waitress to fulfill Selena's drink order.

"Thank you girl, that shit was giving me a headache," Brianna said while searching her purse for an Advil.

"Oh I thought it was the bitch over there with the Hot pink dress from City Trends, with the matching hair, that had your head hurting!" Brianna looked in the direction that Selena was pointing in and both girls immediately started laughing.

"Damn no she didn't put the pink lipstick and eye shadow on too!"

"Yea I guess Walgreen's was having a hellva sale!" Selena managed to get out while holding her stomach in laughter.

"Where in the hell is Charrise? I got to get her to grab a picture of this shit, and post it on her instagram. Both girls looked around in search of Charrise, but were unable to locate her. Charrise was making her way around the whole club making sure that everyone got a good look at her new outfit. Her trot had brought her full circle to the entrance to the club. She had arrived just in time to see the security holding Jonathan and his crew up at the door.

"What's up baby bro?" she yelled so loud that everyone turned in her direction.

"Oh this your people Charrise?" the large light skinned security guard asked in his deep New York accent.

"Yea Big daddy Rah, that's me and Bri's baby brother." Rah turned back towards Jonathan and motion for him and his crew to come forward.

"Next time just say you with Bri and Charrise, don't be talking about you on some list, every nigga tries that lie, lil bro."

Charrise guided Jonathan and his boys to the Vip area where Brianna and Selna where sitting. The guy had made his way back with Selna's drink and decide for himself that he would stay in their booth. Selena was actually taken a liking to him so she didn't protest. Charrise didn't wait for any formal introduction, she walked directly up on him and started interrogating him like he was part of Al qadia and she was with national security.

"So, what's your name?"

"Marcus, but my friends call me Sho..."

"Where you from?" Charrise blurted before he could hardly get the words off his lips.

"I'm from South Charlotte, born and bred."

Charrise turned towards Selena, "I like him and I like them shoes." she whispered.

"His shoes?" Selena looked down to see what was so special about his footwear. She had already noticed the black washed Tru Religion jeans and T shirt he had on with the matching hat. She looked closer to see he had on some black Prada champion low cuts. Huh? She thought to herself, there's nothing special about that.

Charrise, as if she had read Selena's mind, spoke directly into her ear. "Not the style girl, the size." Selena caught on instantly and both of them high fived one another.

"Ughhhhhh!!!!" Rick Ross shouted through the mic. The lights in the club focused in on the area, he and the entire Maybach family filled. It was definitely a bonus to have Meek Mills and Wale there to rock the mic.

"My Rolls-Royce triple black, I'm getcha ho
Balling in the club, bottles like I'm meechi ho
Rozza that's my nickname
Cocaine running in my big vein
Self-made, you just affiliated
I built it ground up, you bought it renovated
Talkin' plenty capers, nothing's been authenticated
Funny you claimin' the same bitch that I'm penetratin'
Hold the bottles up, where my comrades?
Where the fucking felons, where my dogs at?
Uh, I got that Archie Bunker
And it's so white I just might charge you double
I think I'm Big Meech, Larry Hoover

Whippin' work, hallelujah
One nation under God
Real niggas getting money from the fucking start"
Rozza and the crew perform every song off the official MMG mix taped. Everyone danced and partied until the lights came on signaling it was time for the club to close. Selena and Marcus exchanged numbers, while Brianna and Charrise circled Jonathan in a hug.

"Aight! I hope you had a good time!" Brianna said as she kissed him on the cheek.

"Yea!" he shouted still hype from a day of celebration.

"Now you see how your big sisters get it in!" Charrise said.

"Thanks ya'll I really had a good time. And it was nice meeting you Selena," Jonathan said.

"Nice meeting you too," Selena said with a smile.

"Ya'll need me to walk ya'll to the car?"

"We got it," Brianna said as they headed in different directions.

Brianna, Charrise and Selena walked toward the car like they were Charlie's Angels, side by side. The closer they got the more apparent it became that something was terribly wrong. They were almost the last ones to leave the club and the parking lot was nearly empty. Brianna picked up her pace and noticed the car was sitting on flat wheels.

"What the fuck!" she yelled.

Charrise and Selena hurried behind her. They all circled the car in disbelief realizing that someone had gone through the trouble of slashing all of the tires on the car. They heard a car pulling up and expected it was someone trying to help.

Much to her surprise when Brianna turned around to address the helper, she recognized Tiffany's face in a car with two other girls.

Tiffany rolled down her window and said, "you're welcome Bitch!'

With catlike reflexes both Charrise and Selena whipped their heads around to get a good look at the perpetrator. Brianna's body tensed up. She balled up her fist and charged towards the car only to be jerked back by Charrise.

"What the fuck are you doing?" Charrise yelled.

"You see what that bitch did?"

Before Brianna had a chance to respond Selena was opening the car door and pulling Tiffany out by the hair. Tiffany's friends quickly came to her rescue rushing out of the car and breaking the two girls apart. No sooner than they had successfully separated the two, Tiffany ran directly into Brianna at full force knocking her to the cement ground below her. That began an all-out girl fight as Charrise and Selena worked to pull Tiffany off of Brianna with the other girls hot on their trail.

While Tiffany and Brianna brawled on the ground throwing punches and pulling hair Selena turned quickly and pushed both girls down to the pavement. Selena moved fast administering a cocktail of elbows, kicks and punches to the girls. They could barely catch their breath before she was coming back at them.

Charrise continued to struggle to split Brianna and Tiffany. Finally, with the other girls escaping back to the car and tending to their wounds, Selena placed a swift kick to Tiffany's core causing her to release Brianna immediately. She fell back and endured a series of kicks and stomps from a stiletto platform pump. Charrise had to snap Selena out of her fighting trance by screaming her name over and over.

"Selena! Selena! Stop! Selena! That's enough."

As soon as Selena hesitated Tiffany's friend pulled the car just close enough for her to be pulled in. The trio sped off.

By that time Charrise had walked a limping Brianna to the car. There was blood everywhere. Charrise threw the phone to Selena who caught it with one hand while she wasn't even looking.

"Selena call Jonathan and have him come back here and get us. We're going to have to take her to the hospital. Where the fuck is all this blood coming from?" Charrise said as she scanned Brianna's body. There seemed to only be a few scuffs and scratches; nothing that should have caused that much blood.

Simultaneously Brianna and Charrise noticed that the puddle was coming from between her legs. Selena walked back towards the car saying, "Jonathan's on his way. He wasn't that far so he'll be pulling up any minute. Are you o-."

Selena stopped when she noticed all of the blood. "Oh my god! Did she cut you?"

"No," Brianna said while shaking her head. She started feeling cramping in her belly. As soon as Jonathan pulled up they loaded into the car and drove to Carolina's Medical Center to the downtown Emergency room.

Once the Emergency Room nurses noticed all of the blood Brianna was losing they admitted her right away. Charrise held her hand and went to the examination room with her while Jonathan and Selena waited in the lobby. While they waited, Selena called Kacy to catch him up on the eventful night.

"See," Kacy said, "that's exactly why we needed you down here. That broad Tiffany is crazy. I had a feeling she was going to keep trying to start shit."

"Well I damn sure finished it tonight," Selena told him.

"I don't know Selena.... You might have stopped her tonight, but she's the kinda chic that'll keep coming back for more. Especially because there's a lot of money at stake."

Selena nodded intently listening to Kacy when Charrise came back into the lobby.

"She lost the baby in the fight," Charrise explained.

Jonathan contorted his face, "Baby?" he asked.

"Oh no..." Selena said. "Let me call you back K."

"Yeah, she was only two months pregnant. She was already under a lot of stress and I guess this was just the straw that broke the camel's back."

"Damn... I was gonna be an uncle?" Jonathan said.

"Yup... you were. Brianna's not taking it so well. They're going to do a DNC right now, so we have a little time before we can see her. Let's try to get that car towed or something."

Selena chimed in, "Not necessary. I already called Kacy and he's on top of it. He's going to come by here and bring another car for us."

"Aiight," Charrise said with a slight smile, "Jonathan thanks for coming to rescue us. But it's late and you might as well head back home."

"Nah, I'll stay."

Charrise shook her head, "I don't need mom and dad giving you an interrogation when you get home super late. They don't need to know about any of this."

"Not a problem." Jonathan assured her. "Just promise me that you'll call me in the morning."

"I promise." Charrise told him.

Chapter 6

Hakeem looked at his attorney in disbelief. The story he was giving him now was the same story he'd been giving him for the past seven weeks.

"Damn Mr. Randolph."

"What the fuck do you mean, this is the best you can do?" Hakeem asked angrily.

"Mr. Johnson like I've been trying to explain to you for the past couple of weeks now."

"The judge's hands are tied and bound by sentencing guidelines."

"Sentencing guidelines" Hakeem asked.

"Yes."

"Look, Mr. Randolph you're going to have to explain this guideline shit too me, cause I ain't signing no plea agreement for no four hundred and five fuckin months. Not this black-ass nigga right here." He continued fuming.

"Mr. Johnson I have tried everything possible to persuade the district attorney to offer us a more reasonable plea bargain but."

"But what man!"

"But he just won't budge."

Both the attorney and client sat in complete silence a long moment before Hakeem finally spoke.

"Look man, listen we're going to take this shit to trail and beat this shit."

Mr. Randolph slowly nodded his head before responding.

"Hakeem, I know things may sound impossible, but there are

other ways. I just have to be honest with you, going to trial would be suicide. You must not forget that you were caught with three kilo's of crack cocaine son."

"So what exactly are you saying Mr. Randolph?" Hakeem asked him. "And you need to be straight with me too dog."

"I always shoot straight with all my clients Hakeem." His attorney answered sounding a little annoyed by his statement. Hakeem nodded his understanding.

"As I was saying, if we take this to trial it will be your call Hakeem. This is my job I make a living doing this every day so believe me when I say this. I will stand next to you through it all, right by your side Hakeem. I will scratch and fight to do all in my power to win, but if we happen to lose, which I think we will, your life on the streets will be over. Now it's your life and if you want to roll the dice we will. But at the end, only one will be left holding the bank."

Hakeem looked his attorney direct in the eyes and spoke. "I've never left a crap game, and didn't leave with the bank." He smiled then continued, "Put twelve motha-fucka in the box and let's do it."

Twelve months later

"The Aftermath"

Hakeem sat alone inside his cell and for the first time in months he felt liked smiling. After the judge sentenced him to life in prison he was transported to USP Big Sandy Kentucky. He was immediately met by a group of his homeboys from North Carolina. A few were even from his hometown of Charlotte. But behind the wall of prison North Carolina was considered as one. People who usually beefed on the streets were forced to watch each other back 24/7.

As soon as Hakeem got to the pound he was hit with a few rules, but the most important one was his paperwork. It had to be straight or he would have to leave the compound. If he snitched on someone he was subject to be killed on the spot. And that could easily be done by one his own homies. The other rules were simple; no gambling, no drugs, and the most important rule of them all... the no B.B.B. rule! No faggots or what they were referred to on the compound as Big Butt Boys, nasty mothafuckas. Day after day Hakeem would experience something new within the deadly prison walls. Fights, stabbings, and even murder were normal circumstances during everyday prison life, and it took the strongest of men to hold onto not only their sanity but also their manhood.

If you were weak you would fall by the wayside. And once you had failed, it was over. You immediately belonged to whoever wanted you. After only two months Hakeem's mental state was riding on the fringes of insanity. All throughout his years of gangbanging in his neighborhood he'd never seen as much blood as he'd witnessed there. Niggas were getting their heads split wide the fuck open. He'd witnessed several hardcore nigga's having to be rolled out of the shower because they'd been gang raped by undercover faggots plotting the showers at night. Life behind bars was definitely not for the average man. Unable to tolerate it anymore Hakeem contacted his attorney in hopes of working out a deal with the district attorney in his case. After many calls, debriefings, and sleepless nights his attorney was able to convince the D.A. to allow his client to become a cooperating witness. Hakeem was so happy about the possibility of reducing his life sentence that he accidentally let his guard down and it nearly cost him his life.

"Damn nigga you playin that mail call close," Hakeem's cell-mate said to him.

"Yea I'm waitin on some legal mail play-boy," Hakeem answered.

"Legal mail?"

"Yeah legal mail nigga."

"Mothafucka yo blackass got life just like me."

"What's that supposed to mean?"

"It mean that you gon die in here nigga that's what tha fuck it mean."

"Nah nigga..I'm bout too…" Hakeem cut his last statement off.

"What was that Hakeem? What was you about to say?"

"Never mind nigga. Never mind." he said again before walking out the small cell heading towards the T.V. room. The next several days went by with Hakeem acting strangely to all his homies in his cell block. Most of them had already been down for a decade or more and they knew all the signs of someone who was about to crash and burn. A couple of days later Hakeem had gotten caught up on the rec yard and was forced to miss legal mail call. After the rec yard was finally opened he rushed to the unit in hopes of catching the officer over the mail before they left.

"Damn!" he mumbled when he walked in and realized the officer had already come and gone. He walked to his cell to prepare for a shower. As soon as he stepped into his cell block he was met by a barrage of violent blows. Hakeem's survival instincts immediately kicked in and he began swinging wildly in all directions. But the blows he threw had little to no effect on his attackers. Then one solid punch to his temple brought him down and the last thing he remembered was the voice of his cellmate yelling.

"You fuckin bitch-ass snitch nigga turn that motha-fucka over on his stomach."

Hakeem didn't even have time to panic before a dark shade of blackness veiled over his eyes. The next day Hakeem awoke in the prison informatory. Luckly for him it was time for the CO on duty to make their rounds. The CO was able to call for back up before Hakeem suffered too much damage or possibly death.

"Damn that was close, "Hakeem said shaking himself from his thoughts. He stood up and walked over to the small mirror on the dingy wall. He began examining the bruises all over his face. The following day he was in transit, on his way back to the Charlotte Mecklenburg County Jail where he would be interviewed by several agents over different cases around Charlotte and surrounding counties.

Chapter 7

Early on a Saturday morning, Charrise sat on the chaise lounge in the media room catching up on VH1s Basketball Wives. She'd gotten out of her bed and went immediately to the TV. It was her sole goal on that day to empty her DVR of all the show's she'd missed over the last few weeks. Her eyes were glued to the television as yet another girl fight was about to commence. As stupid as she thought those women were, arguing and fighting over gossip and men, she had to laugh at the fact that recently the things going on in her inner circle were beginning to look like the makings of a reality television show. She suddenly felt a familiar buzz on her thigh. Charrise looked down at her vibrating phone. An image of her mother smiling with her hair styled in a salt and pepper doobie appeared on the screen.

"Hey Mama," Charrise chimed as she answered the phone.

"Hey baby," Lorraine said in a murmur.

"Why are you talking so low? I can barely hear you."

"Your father is asleep and I don't want to wake him."

"Ok… what's up?" Charrise could tell something was wrong. Herman was known for getting down right belligerent if anyone woke him up out of his sleep. It didn't make any since that she'd be making the call with him asleep and only a few feet away.

"I need your help…. I mean we… we need your help."

"I can't give ya'll no more money than I been doing Ma."

"It's serious baby. He's in the hospital again."

It was at that moment that Charrise noticed the steady beeping in the back ground.

" Again?"

"I didn't want to worry you. But I think you should know that things aren't looking good for him."

"What's going on? He seemed fine the last time I saw him…. Mean, but healthy."

"You didn't notice how much weight he gained and how bad his skin looked."

Charrise felt guilty because she hadn't. She hadn't had a lot of interaction with him since she'd moved out. She generally met with her mom to give them money. When she spoke to him on the phone she rushed him, when she saw him he was almost always drunk so she avoided him.

Lorraine continued, "You kids get grown and all but forget that you have parents at all. I'm not surprised that you didn't notice."

"Ma…" Charrise started, remorse coating her words, "It's not like that… I've just…"

"Been busy. I know. I know. You tell me that all the time. I just want you to know what's going on with your father. You should tell Brianna too."

"I don't think she'll really care, but ok."

"Herman's the only father she's ever known. She should know how bad things are getting… and that we're damn near drowning in medical debt. I just don't know how long I can keep this going."

Charrise could hear the stress and sorrow in her mother's voice. Tears started to fill up in her eyes. She wiped on just before it spilled out. "Well you said you need some help. What do you want me to do?"

Just as the words entered her mouth, Brianna sashayed into the room wearing leggings and a tee shirt that clung to her skin with fuzzy slippers on her feet. "Who's that," she asked with suspicious look on her face.

Charrise cupped the phone, "It's mama."

Brianna shook her head, "What does she want now? She better not be asking for more money."

Charrise put her finger up to hush her sister and started back listening to her mother's voice, "He has cirrhosis of the liver… I think he's going to end up needing a transplant."

"We'll Ma, I only have one liver so I can't help you there."

Brianna scrunched up her face, "What? A liver? You've got to be kidding me."

"Hold on a sec Mama," Charrise cupped her hand over the phone for a second time, "So apparently daddy has cirrhosis of the liver."

Brianna was indignant, "Why am I not surprised?"

"Look sis, I know you hate him, but he's still my dad."

"You know I know that… and I wish I could be a bigger person and feel even a little bit bad for him…. But…"

"I know. You don't. I tried to tell Mama that. Let me finish up with her real quick." Charrise put the phone back to her ear, "I'm back. So I can't give him a liver, but what else can I do."

"We'll it's like what I was telling you earlier…. I don't know how long we can keep paying these hospital bills."

"What about your insurance?"

"We had to cut back once things started going downhill at the restaurants. We don't have decent coverage. Bills are starting to mount."

"Ma, I already give ya'll a lot of money every month."

Lorraine exhaled loudly into the phone, "I know baby. And we really appreciate it. But if you could just do a little more.."

"I'll see what I can do Ma."

"Maybe your sist…"

"Don't even go there. She's not hearing it… AT ALL."

"Ok, well if nothing else you could at least come check on him more often."

"I can do that for sure. Look I gotta go. I'ma se what I can work out for you and I'll give you a call back later, ok?"

"Ok baby. I love you."

"I love you too."

When Charrise got off the phone Brianna was sitting in a chair across the room in her standard mad stance. Arms and legs crossed. The top leg bobbing up and down fast.

"I'm not going to let you give them any more money Charrise."

"B, I'm grown. I can do what I want with my money!"

"This just don't make no sense. You should haven't to take care of him. Especially not after the way he came at you the last time."

"But he's really sick."

"Weren't you the one telling me about how his drinking was getting out of control. Didn't you even say he was drunk at Jonathan's graduation cookout. That wasn't that long ago Charisse. What would be the point of you giving extra money so he can get healthy, just so he can keep drinking and let it all go to waste anyway."

"So I'm just supposed to sit back and not do anything."

"Like you said, you're grown... I can't tell you what to do with your money... but you need to consider this. Why would you be doing more to benefit his health than he's doing for himself. He's still drinking even though he knows he has this condition.... I wouldn't give him a damn thing."

Chapter 8

Hakeem sat alone inside the holding cell just outside the main courtroom. His adrenaline was still pumping from the testimony he'd just given on his latest trail case.

"Shit nigga you could have won a Oscar wit dat one." He said to himself. "Damn," he said again now thinking about the immediate release he'd been promised if the courts got a conviction with his testimony. Well they got that conviction and even better for the DA, all four defendants had received three life sentences. Hakeem never thought twice about the fact that one of those convictions was a woman with four kids, that he once considered a friend.

"Here I come motha-fuckas! Yea here I fuckin come. That nigga bout to be back on the block!" he screamed pumping his fist in the air.

Hakeem's lawyer filed two separate motions on his behalf. A motion for reduction in sentence, because he gave the government substantial assistance, and he also filed a S.K.I. motion asking for immediate release. For the next three weeks Hakeem paced the floor of his cell day and night. Whenever he did decide to sleep visions of Brianna flooded his thoughts like never before.

That's why the bitch was acting the way she was, he thought. Hakeem had finally figured out why those three extra kilos were placed in his package. Brianna had planned it. She knew I would take the bait. Damn that was stupid!" Hakeem shouted out mad at himself. Then he gave a grim-lined smile.

"But bitch I'ma hit you where it really hurts." He mumbled with

51

thoughts of Brianna and her little sister Charrise running through his head.

Hakeem didn't sleep a wink that night. He just kept walking around in circles in his tiny cell. His lawyer had assured him that he would be out shortly after shift change. So he was watching the clock waiting on 7:00am.

"Mr. Johnson, are you ready?" Hakeem's lawyer asked, breaking him from his thoughts.

"What kinda motherfucking question is that? Hell yea I'm ready!"

"Well you just have to go through the standard release procedures and I will meet you downstairs."

It was a Tuesday morning so processing went quickly. He shook Mr. Randolph's hand and walked outside into the fresh Charlotte morning air, a free man. He was immediately greeted with a hug and kiss from Tiffany.

"I missed you so much babe. It's about to be on and popping now that you back. I got a big welcome home party lined up for you tonight at club Nikki's. The whole city coming out!"

"That's what's up, where you parked at? I'm trying to get as far away from this place as fast as possible." Hakeem responded while walking towards the parking deck. When they arrived at the car Hakeem instructed Tameka to give him the keys.

"Let me drive, while you take care of a nigga."

"What you mean Hakeem?" Tiffany asked, while entering the passenger side of the car and fasting her seatbelt.

"Go ahead and handle the situation for a nigga," he responded, looking at his already erected dick, pulsating threw his pants.

"Hakeem its broad daylight out here and we in a public place, you can't wait till we get home. I can really take care of you then daddy!" She said trying to sound convincing.

"Look that's all good but, just take care of this for right now," Hakeem didn't wait for her acceptance of his statement, instead he grabbed the back of Tiffany's head and pushed it into his crotch while pulling his rock hard penis out at the same time. Tiffany sucked her teeth in disapproval, but did as she was told and began sucking and slurping like she had a double dipped cone from Dairy Queen.

Hakeem sat back enjoying the whole scene. He had visualized this sight in his mind, over and over while locked up and now here he was. It didn't take long for Hakeem to bust off. He held Tiffany's head tightly against his mid-section, while his dick filled her mouth with cum. His head fell back against the head rest.

"Damn I really did miss you, that was some good shit!" he gasped out.

"Not half as good as it's going to be when I get you home." Tiffany responded after swallowing a mouth full semen.

That night Hakeem sat inside Club Nikki's. Tameka didn't lie everyone in the city was at the hottest strip club in Charlotte. He glanced at his Rolex watch then silently cursed under his breath.

"Can I get you another drink?" Asked an almost nude waitress interrupting his thoughts.

Hakeem didn't answer right away—instead he checked out her skimpy attire, which consisted of a thin black wife-beater cut off barley below the bottom of her breast. Stretched across the thin material were the words Nikki's.

"Nice shirt," he said, forgetting her question and eyeing her two beautifully erect nipples. "What's the occasion?"

"Oh, you haven't heard?"

"Nah I haven't."

"Damn nigga where you been , under a rock or cum'en?" She spat, then rolled her eyes towards the ceiling before continuing. Well anyway, this is a homecoming."

"Yeah".

"Hell yeah!"

"Alright cool—I'll take that drink," he requested, then dug into his pocket---only to be stopped by her.

"Oh no suga… all drinks are on the house , compliments of Havoc."

"That's whasup shawty..this for you then." He said giving her a twenty dollar bill.

"I'll be at the bar if you need anything—and I do mean A-N-Y-T-H-I-N-G", she stressed before turning to leave.

"What's yo' name shawty?" Hakeem asked.

"I'm sorry—call me Stormy."

"Stormy", he asked as if wondering where she got a name like that from.

Like she had just read his mind she responded "Yes stormy because I can definitely make it come up a cloud—all you have to do is make it rain nigga."

"What's yo name anyway?"

"Hakeem… but you can just call me Havoc." He said with a sly smile.

"O, I'm so sorry I didn't know you where the man of the hour." She grinned, then turned and strutted towards the bar.

After getting his drink Hakeem focused his attention on the many posters, fliers, and photo's hanging throughout the club. Tiffany had really out done herself. But right now he had other things on his mind.

"Damn," Hakeem mumbled everything was going according to his plan, except for the fact that his nigga was late! Hakeem turned to the door, just as Tank, also known around the city as Biggie, because of his resemblance, walked in. Tank really made one understand the big, black and ugly, the famous rapper had spoken about.

"Damn nigga..what tha fuck took you so long?" Hakeem complained when Tank finally sat down next to him.

"I called yo' fat black ass over two hours ago!" he continued.

"Chill wit that fat boy shit!" Tank said getting aggressive over the name calling.

Hakeem could see his body twitching uncontrollably and knew instantly that tank was high.

"Nigga you caked tha fuck up ain't chu" Hakeem asked.

"I did a couple lines my nigga, but I'm good."

"What's popping?" he asked.

"I've got something I want to put you up on, but I got to know you going to keep your mind straight. And that means chilling on that nose candy my nigga," Hakeem said his voice turning serious.

"Don't you worry about me bro, I got this under control. Now let's hear what you got for me" Tank said already knowing more than likely it was some grimy shit.

Tiffany had come over and sat on the other side of Hakeem and begun sipping on a long island ice tea, she was trying her best to make out their conversation, but could barely hear them.

Tank stared at his partner in crime in disbelief, his mouth went dry, and he took a quick sip of his drink before he finally responded.

"Nigga are you serious?"

"Dead serious Tank... Dead fucking serious."

"Damn Hakeem." After a long moment of silence tank asked, ""Are you sure want to do this?"

Hakeem didn't answer right away. Bitterness seeped through his veins exiting his pores as his mind once again returned to Brianna. He'd pay her back he continued thinking. He would never let a woman beat him at his own game!

"Hakeem," Tank called, interrupting his thoughts.

"What is it nigga?" Hakeem asked sourly.

"I asked you was you sure about this?"

"Do I look like I'm bull-shitting wit chu nigga?"

"Well I can tell you now we going to need some help with this and with the word being out about you fucking around with the FEDS it's going to be hard to get crewed up!"

"Nigga can't none of that shit be confirmed on these streets and mutherfucker's are starving right now so for the right amount of bread they will forget all that shit. So you let me worry about that, you just find a nigga to rock with you for what I need you to handle and I will take care of the rest.

"Shit I already got someone in mind" Tank answered.

"Who?" Hakeem asked looking at the smirk Tank had formed on his fat face.

"Cowboy, who else?"

"That old nigga bro? How you going to get Unk down with some shit like this?"

"Yea that old nigga, you know he murder certified and he needs the money, so I know he will be down. And best of all he don't deal with no young nigga's so I don't have to worry about discussing your street rep right now...."

Hakeem cut him off, "Look for the last time don't keep bringing up that shit, a nigga had do what a nigga had to do to make sure I could see these streets again. I didn't fuck nobody who I rocked with, so to me it's a dead issue. And if somebody got a problem with it

Fuck'em. Now don't blow a nigga high at my homecoming party. If I was your black ass I would be finding one of these strippers broke enough to want to buff that little black dick of yours off!" Hakeem said trying to hold back his laughter.

"Fuck you nigga, but I will take another one of these drinks, since it's all on you!"

Hakeem partied the night away and just like he predicted one by one nigga's was coming up to him congratulating him on making it back on the streets and asking for him to hook them up. Hakeem understood that at the end of the day the streets had to be fed and when they were hungry they really didn't pay attention to the hand that was feeding them as long as the food kept coming.

On the drive home Hakeem and Tiffany discussed her run in with Brianna at the club.

"Yeah your bitch trying to act like she got heart now. Her and her girls tried to jump me outside of Lux, but you know me and my girls sent them bitches packing. She do got one chick riding with her that can fight, but you know I put her on her ass!" Tiffany said giving her version of the events.

"Well I don't care who she got with her, that's shit going to get handle. But for right now I need for you to just fall back on this beef with her. I got some real shit planned for her and her sista ass."

"What you going to do Hakeem, tell me?" Tiffany pleaded.

"Na... not right now, but just know your nigga going to be back on top and you going to be right there with me!" Hakeem knew exactly what to say to make Tiffany happy. She smiled and laid her head back in the seat.

****

Brianna drove into her old parking garage at a cautious pace with Kacy and Selena in the back seat. The darkly tinted windows held her identity incognito. Still she felt a severe sense of unease flow all around her. Two days ago she'd been informed by her tenant at her and Tre's old home that FBI agents had come by with several questions pertaining to her whereabouts. After which there was an unmarked car parked in front of the condos watching the building. Before exiting the charcoal gray rented suburban Selena spoke.

"Hey Bri, let me go inside and check things out mami."

Before answering Brianna craned her neck in all directions, for any signs of someone laying and waiting, or watching for that matter.

"Did you hear me Bri?" Selena asked her again.

"Ye...yea....I mean yes.

"Are you saying yes as to you hear me, or yes I want you to go inside to check things out?"

"Oh I'm sorry Selena... Yes, please check it out."

Without hesitation, Selena exited the SUV then disappeared into the lobby of the building.

Within minutes she came back to the car and escorted Brianna to the elevator. Angie, Brianna's tenant came to the door. Once inside Angie filled Brianna in on all the questions the federal officer's had asked, as well as what they looked like. Brianna tried her best to hide her nervousness, but did a poor job because her right foot was steadily tapping on the floor.

The conversation left Brianna thoroughly confused. The feds had gone to her old residence simply to determine her whereabouts. Nothing else. They simply wanted to know where she was laying her head.

"But why?" she began thinking," why would the feds be asking questions about her?"

Brianna retracted all of her most recent problems with different wanna be thugs she'd had run-ins with, most of whom were connected to her by Hakeem. She felt confident that she'd covered any and everything that could trace any wrong doings back to her.

Kacy could see the tension on Brianna's face so he cut into her thoughts.

"Look Bri, they just wanted to know where you were, that's all. It could be something as simple as them having some information about Tre's death. So don't let this shit get to you. What we need to do is reach out to an attorney and let them see what's real.

"You right Kasy, and I know just who to call." Brianna spoke with confidence.

She had made the decision to call someone she was familiar with Tre's old attorney. Tre had sent her by his office plenty of times to drop off money. How had she forgotten to make sure she stayed lawyered up as Tre referred to it. He had always made sure he kept at least one attorney on retainer.

****

"Greetings Brianna it's been a while." Tre's old attorney said, extending his hand to her.

"Yes it has been quite some time." Brianna said to him.

"Now if I may ask, what brings you to my office today?"

"Well Mr. Casteno, I think I may have a problem, a big problem." Brianna said.

"Oh I see, well what kind of problem are we talking about?"

"The feds kinda problem." Brianna then said.

At the mention of the name feds, Mr. Casteno leaned forward in his chair, he spoke.

"Yes that can be a huge problem, please tell me everything you know, and do not leave any details out."

Brianna nodded her head in understanding then gathered her thoughts before giving him all the details. Once she finished Brianna sat patiently in front of Mr. Casteno, waiting on some type of response. She felt as if his lake blue eyes where penetrating through her as he stared calmly in her direction. After a long moment he spoke.

"Brianna, let's just make the very first assumption clear." He paused, and then continued, "the feds are looking for you, the question is why? Why do they want to know your whereabouts? If they were questioning people down at the headquarters, that would be different, but instead there looking into all of your previous addresses."

"All of them?" Brianna asked in surprise.

"Yes, all of them, and I'm sure they even have checked out your mother and father's address."

"Damn!" Brianna said loudly.

"It's nothing to be too worried about, when I say checked, it doesn't mean they necessarily went there, in fact I'm almost certain that they only surveyed the home in hopes of seeing you."

"Damn." Brianna mumbled again, relieved that she hadn't stopped by her parents' house during her younger brother Jonathan's graduation party.

"Is there anything... anything else you can think of, that might be helpful?"

"No Mr. Casteno, I can't think of anything else."

"Very well, I'll get right on this. In the meantime just stick to your normal everyday activities, my honest opinion is that if the federal government wanted you for something major, then there is no doubt that you would be behind bars. So until I have more for you, don't you sweat this at all ok?"

"Ok, thank you so much Mr. Casteno" Brianna shook his hand and headed out the door.

Brianna pulled out her phone and saw there were several missed calls and texted. She walked towards the elevator while scrolling through her messages. Just as she rounded the corner of the elevators she walked directly into a chest that smelled of Gucci cologne. When she looked up, she met familiar eyes.

"Brianna?" the voice bellowed towards her.

Brianna smiled and tucked her hair behind her ear, "Oh my god. I'm so sorry!"

"It's quite alright. No need to apologize."

Brianna continued to smile getting lost in the chestnut colored eyes that gazed at her.

"It's good to see you again," he said.

"You too. You work here?"

"Yeah, I've been an attorney for about 10 years now."

"Good for you. I was just handling some legal matters for my business. I didn't expect to run into my neighbor."

"You know... I actually wouldn't mind running into you a bit more often." He said with a cool smile and mellow voice.

Brianna couldn't help but smile like a school girl. She rubbed her hand across his shoulder as she walked towards the elevator, "We'll just have to make that happen now won't we." She pressed the button for the elevator and could feel his eyes looming over her. She couldn't blame him. She wore a black skirt suit that was anything but basic. The jacket stopped just below her waist, and the skirt clung to her curves putting her best asset on display.

When the elevator arrived and Brianna stepped on Brandon was right on her heels entering with her.

"Let me take you to dinner some time." He said.

Brianna pushed the button for the ground floor before responding, "Sure." She said simply.

"Are you busy this weekend?"

"I'll have to check, but I think I'm free."

Brandon walked Brianna to her car and they exchanged numbers. As she sat in her car alone beaming about her upcoming date, she couldn't help but to think about Tre. She could barely remember their first date. The thought of having a first date with her neighbor made her nervous. What if she didn't like him after the date? She thought. Would things be weird when she saw him in the street?

It was at that moment that Brianna realized that she was entering yet another new phase in her life. Tre's death had brought about more changes than she could have ever imagined. Dating. The idea of it intrigued her. She'd never really had the opportunity to do that in the past. She was practically clueless on how these things even worked. Brianna had moved in with Tre shortly after they'd started dating. The only other man she was close to was Hakeem, and she still got sick to her stomach when she thought of him. Still she didn't regret the decisions she'd made or the experiences she'd had.

Brianna had been like any other young girl with dreams of growing up, getting married, having babies, working a normal job and living happily ever after. It was the first day since Tre's murder that she considered that it might not be too late for that.

She pushed those feelings back and told herself, "One step at a time Brianna."

Brianna put the keys in the ignition and headed home.

****

Hakeem had been back on the street of Charlotte for a few weeks lying low. He hadn't left Tiffany's house since the homecoming party. After days of hiding out, Hakeem began to gather his thoughts and put together a plan. A plan that would get him back into the upper player status of the streets and ultimately allow him to bring down one of the most under the radar female Drug King-pins in the city of Charlotte's history.

But Hakeem also knew the first matter at hand concern him, and his now severely tarnished street credibility. Stepping on the wrong grounds in and around the Charlotte area could instantly get him killed. He snatched up his cheap Verzion pre-paid cell phone. He knew the last thing he needed was to catch a new case from running his mouth on a phone in his own name. After turning the power on he breathed a sigh of relief after seeing that he did have a signal. He punched in some numbers and then waited.

"Agent Ross." A man said on the end of the line.

"Yo Ross this is..."

"My main man Hakeem!" Agent Ross cut him off saying.

"We were told down at the station that you had been released and would be contacting us."

"What else were you told?" Hakeem asked, already knowing the answer to his own question.

"We were also told you are a marked man Hakeem, your days of walking the streets in this city could be numbered."

"I hear you, I hear you...... I hear you!" Hakeem cut agent Ross off with a shout saying.

He continued. "Look... Listen up man... I need some help."

"What type of help are we talking about Hakeem? And what are you willing to give up or sacrifice to get that help?"

"How about a body and some major dope?" Hakeem stated matter-of- factly.

"A body and drugs?" Agent Ross said in surprise.

"Not only a body and drugs... but a body, drugs and a suspect with it all red handed."

Agent Ross let out a low whistle before responding, "I like that."

"How soon can we meet?" agent Ross than asked.

"Meet me behind the old Eastland mall building off Central." Hakeem said, now giving orders.

"I'll be there in an hour." Agent Ross said.

After his meeting with the Feds Hakeem was back at Tiffany's. When he pulled up he was glad to see that she hadn't gotten back home yet. Tiffany was always asking a bunch of questions and Hakeem knew that the less she knew what he was up to, the better. The meeting with Agent Ross and his partner had gone off just as he hoped. The officer's knew his information would be of use to the homicide division down at the station. And the drugs case would be one that would put them on the six o'clock news. Also before his release from prison he'd given them some very credible information on a female trap-star by the name of Brianna Campbell. Top agents down at the station followed up on the information given to them and the investigation quickly turned into a red hot case. Hakeem removed his sticky clothes before jumping into the shower. After showering he pulled on a fresh white wife beater and pair of true religion jeans that sagged halfway down his ass. He concealed his 41 millimeter pistol with little effort then gave himself a quick inspection in the mirror on the bedroom wall. After giving himself his own seal of approval, he smiled.

"It's time for a nigga to get the fuck up outta here and clear his mother-fucking name up." Hakeem mumbled.

Reaching behind the flimsy headboard of the bed he opened a small digital safe, reached inside and grabbed five stacks. After another quick glance, he turned and walked out of the apartment. Tiffany had not been able to keep up the payments on his cars. So he was force to drive around in a 2002 Honda Accord that he use to deliver dope in. Hakeem made a mental not to himself. That he would have to grab something fly real soon before too many people saw him in the compact car.

Chapter 9

The sound of the doorbell sent the sound of a chime through the house. Both Selena and Charrise's heads snapped and turned towards the door. They giggled like school girls. Charrise's jaw had dropped when Brianna told her that she'd ran into the sexy neighbor, and that he'd asked her out on a date.

"You know what," she'd said, "I'm not even surprised. I knew it would only be a matter of time before he asked you out the way he was looking at you that day. The real surprise is that you actually said yes."

Brianna had scrunched up her face, "Why you say that?"

Charrise shrugged, "I always thought you liked thugs. This is a true pretty boy."

Brianna couldn't exactly dispute that claim considering her track record. But one thing she knew for sure was that she was ready for a change when it came to men. By her estimate, it was high time to have a man with as little drama as possible. Brandon seemed to be the perfect match for the job… so far.

"Your date's here!" Charrise yelled upstairs.

"Can somebody get that please?" Brianna yelled back.

Charrise rushed to the door and opened up quickly, "Hello," she said, "Come on in."

Brandon looked like he'd fallen right off the pages of a J Crew catalog. He wore a grey two button blazer over a stripped tee shirt that he'd paired with dark denim jeans. He walked in and his signature fragrance wafted into Charrise's nostrils.

"Dayam," she mouthed to Selena as he strolled past her further into the house.

"So what do you ladies have planned for the night," Brandon asked trying to fill the awkward silence in the room.

"Nothing much," Charrise said while taking him by the hand and pulling him into the living room. "We'll probably just watch some TV and wait up on Brianna so she can give us all the juicy details of your date!"

Brandon smiled in response.

"You know," Selena added with a smile of her own, "Girl stuff."

Brianna entered the living room wearing an outfit that nearly took Brandon's breath away. It was just the type of understated sexy that he liked. She wore teal skinny jeans with a nearly sheer tunic that hung off of her right shoulder. Her hair was pulled back into a low ponytail that fell between her shoulders in soft curls. Brianna's lips shined of gloss and her eye shadow glimmered when she blinked. She carried a small golden clutch purse that matched her platform hills.

"I'm ready. Are you?" she asked Brandon.

Brandon stood up, and his eyes glazed over her in admiration. He walked over her way and reached out for a hug. Brianna kindly accepted his gesture with a soft squeeze in return.

Outside Brandon's BMW 6 series coupe glistened in the setting sun. He rushed ahead of Brianna, making sure that her hands would not have to touch the door. She appreciated his efforts to be a gentleman. Although Tre had taken very good care of her, a gentleman he was not.

Once inside the car she noted that he kept it just as shiny and clean on the inside as he did the outside. As they drove towards South Park Mall, Brandon took some time getting to know Brianna.

"Are you from Charlotte?"

"Yeah, born and raised."

"Wow… that's a rarity. Most people here are transplants."

"I get that all the time. How about you?"

"I grew up here. But I'm from a small town called Greenville. What high school did you go to?"

"East Meck. You?" Brianna smiled as she followed the rules

to this familiar conversation. It was one of those discussions that always helped break the ice between two strangers attempting to find common ground.

"Garinger. I had friends that went to East though, what year'd you graduate?"

"2004." She answered.

He grinned, "So that means you're around 25 or 26."

"Was that you're way of trying to figure out how old I am?" she said with a side eye.

"Kinda." He laughed, "But I was also just trying to get to know you.

Before she could respond they pulled up to Cowfish near South Park Mall, and Brianna was excited. She loved sushi and had wanted to try the restaurant, but hadn't gotten around to it yet. As they parked Brianna reached for the door, only to be interrupted.

"I'll get that for you," Brandon said as he jumped out of the car and met her on the passenger side to let her out.

At the entrance of the restaurant Brandon and Brianna were greeted by the hostess, "Welcome to Cowfish," she said with a smile. "Two people tonight?"

"Yes," Brandon said.

"Ok, now there's a twenty minute wait. Is that okay?"

Brandon looked over to Brianna and asked, "Is that ok."

Brianna simply nodded as she looked past Brandon into the interior of the restaurant. The place was lively and bright, filled with 3-d art and pops of color. She noticed the shelfes lined decoratively with ketchup and soy sauce on some and the combination of soy sauce and mustard on others.

The hostess handed Brandon the buzzer and the two headed outside to wait. Brianna walked a few steps ahead of Brandon and stopped once she found some free space to linger. As soon as she turned around Brandon said, "Did I mention how beautiful you look tonight?"

Brianna beamed. She relished in this simple compliment that was so much different from the normal, 'Damn baby you thick', or 'You're so goddamn sexy'.

The bright red walls and pop art had a fun and trendy feel.

"Thank you." She replied, "But don't think that made me forget about you trying to sneak and ask my age."

"So I guess it's only fair I reveal my age." He said.

"Naw... let me ask you in the same sneaky way you asked me," she flirted.

"Aiight, go ahead."

"What year did you graduate from Garinger Brandon? I have sooooo many friends that went there, maybe you know some." She exaggerated.

"I doubt it," he replied.

"Why is that?"

"I graduated a few years before you."

"Ok, I had older friends," she lied. She didn't have many friends at all in high school. And the ones that she did have, weren't any older than her.

"I graduated in '98." He revealed.

"Okay, okay," she said calculating his age in her mind. "Making you 32?"

"Ding ding ding!" he yelled, "And the winner of Guess That Age is Brianna!"

She chuckled, finding his corny joke amusing. The buzzer in Brandon's hand began to vibrate and light up.

"That's us," he said leading the way back to the doors of Cowfish.

They pair was seated in a booth near the bar of the restaurant. They each flip back and forth through the pages of the menu trying to decide what they wanted to order.

"I think I'm going to try something new tonight." Brianna announced.

"You've been here before?"

"No," she said indifferently.

"You've never had sushi before?"

With a scrunched up face she responded, "Of course I have!"

"Then what do you mean you're going to try something new?"

"I've never had burgushi before," she said with a smile.

"Ahhh haaa, which one?"

"The deliverance roll sounds yummy. I like trying new things."

"Is that right?" Brandon asked.

"Yeah, kinda like going out with you."

Brandon laughed, "What's that supposed to mean."

Brianna shrugged before saying, "I usually go for guys who are a little rougher around the edges."

"And I'm not?"

"Ahhh…" Brianna started just as the server returned to the table to take their food orders.

Brianna had never felt more normal that she did on that night. Having pointless conversation about age, school and food choices rather than family drama or illegal activities felt good.

After completing their orders, Brandon said, "Now tell me what makes you think I'm not a rough neck."

Brianna couldn't help but to laugh, "The fact that you're saying rough neck at all but proves my point." she uttered.

"Ok, so you're judging me because I'm not current on my street terminology."

"Don't get me wrong," she said while she continued to laugh. "it's not a bad thing."

"I'll give you that. I'm not rough around the edges… but I'm also not a square," he explained.

Brianna nodded, "It'll be up to you to prove that to me."

"That mean I get another date then?" Brandon asked.

"If it's the only way for me to get to the bottom of whether you're a square or not, I'm in."

"I'd been waiting of the perfect chance to say something to you, but the time never seemed right. It didn't seem real when we ran into each other at my office."

Brianna cringed inside. She hadn't stopped to think about what Brandon might think of her going to see an attorney. She wondered if attorney-client privilege would prevent her own attorney from sharing her personal details with Brandon. She wondered if he'd even asked.

"Yeah, work stuff," she managed to murmur.

"Well you've got yourself one hell of an attorney." He said with a smile.

"Oh yeah?" she asked, trying to see how much he knew about her.

"Definitely! He's a well rounded guy, one of the best in the firm. But I'm sure you know that already. What kind of business are you into?" He asked.

Brianna kicked herself for not preparing a response to this line of questioning. In hindsight, she knew that this would come up, but she'd been so focused on other things about the date.

"Well…" she said hesitating, "I'm a pharmaceutical sales rep. But I'm working on opening a company of my own."

It wasn't a straight out lie, she thought to herself. Plus she'd always considered what opening her own business eventually. The only thing was that she hadn't quite figured out what business would be yet.

"Is that right? Young and ambitious, I can respect that!" Brandon replied.

"It is," she said with a smile, "But right now, I'm not really telling too many people about it because I'm still in the planning phases. I just needed a lawyer to look over some of the preliminary paperwork to make sure I'm on the right track and doing things the right way, ya know?"

"I get it. In other words, that's not something you want to share with me right now."

"Don't take it like that. We barely know each other," she said with a laugh.

"And let me reiterate… tonight we change that!"

Brianna and Brandon made it through their main course with Brianna being overly honest about her upbringing. That was the only part of her life that she could talk to Brandon about without worrying that he'd run in the opposite direction of her. Almost everything in her life that happened after she'd met and moved in with Tre was top secret.

On the walk back to the car Brandon said, "I know you're sister and friend are back at house waiting on you. But I don't want to take you home just yet."

"To be honest, I'm not quite ready to go back yet either," she said while bumping him slightly on the shoulder.

"I'm happy to hear that. Did I pass the square test tonight?"

"I'd give you a B plus tonight." She responded.

Brandon stopped mid-step gave Brianna a hug before saying, "That's passing."

She squeezed her arms tightly around his neck as he held her around her petite waist. She looked up at him and said, "Maybe next time you'll get an A."

"I'll work on that," he replied.

Brianna put her head down, and he tilted it right back up towards him while leaning down to give her a kiss. She freely accepted his soft lips and moist tongue and she felt a familiar tingle between her thighs. She squirmed a bit before pulling away.

"Damn," she mumbled under her breath.

"What's that?" Brandon asked with a slight grin.

"Nothing," she stammered. Brianna could already feel her panties getting wet from that brief kiss. She pulled away and said, "Thanks for taking me out tonight."

Brandon made the few short steps towards the car, letting Brianna inside and closing the door behind her. On the drive home, Brianna pulled out her phone for the first time that night to see she'd missed several calls and texts from Charrise. Her heart began to race with nervous energy as she scrolled through the messages and realized that while she was out having a good time a crisis was going on.

****

"Be back in this house by 2:00 a.m. Jonathan." He heard his mother say to his back as he headed for the door.

Like most guys his age who'd begun to smell themselves, he smacked his teeth at her request. His father's baritone voice intervened.

"Did you hear your mother boy?"

"Yes dad." Jonathan quickly answered, knowing that he couldn't give the same response to Herman.

"Good cause if you don't have your ass back hear by 2 o'clock, you will be answering to me. Is that clear?"

"Yes sir." Jonathan answered.

"Alright then, enjoy yourself." His father finally said.

"And honey please be careful." His mother shouted.

"I will mom." Jonathan said, before walking out the door.

"Come on Lorain, that boy has got to grow up sometime."

"Yes, I know that but he is our last one you know, our last baby bird to leave our nest."

"I know that Lorain, now would you please go to sleep, if not then please allow me to...I feel like shit" he continued.

"Well Herman if you'd stop...."

"Don't start with the lectures tonight Lorain, I'll drink when I damn well please!" he shouted before turning his back to her. Lorain stared at her husband's broad back and shoulders a long moment, then turned her body in the opposite direction of him and prayed a silent prayer for him and her son.

****

"Let me see your I.D's" the big larger than life security guard said to the three young men at the entrance of the club. Each of the young men fumbled through their pockets until they each found their identification. The guard looked at the identifications, then back at each one of them. He repeated the same gesture three times before he said, "This ain't neither one of you lil motha-fucka's, now turn around and take ya'll lil young asses out of here before I..."

The big bouncer's words were cut off by the shortest one standing in the middle who produced three one hundred dollar bills from his pocket.

"Just give us two hours and the money is yours big fella" he said.

The bouncer looked around making sure no one else was within earshot. He spoke

"Guess it's you three little niggas lucky night." He reached out and grabbed the bills, then continued "Two hours...Two hours and ima walk through this club and if I see any of you little nigga's still here... I will personally throw you out myself; now get the fuck inside the club because your time started five minutes ago."

Hakeem sat alone at a table sipping on a glass of lime and Ciroc. He checked his diamond encrusted watch for the time, then smiled at the thought of simply having the expensive watch on his arm. Four months ago he'd damn near forgotten about the watch or any other jewelry he had purchased. The only thing that had mattered was trying to survive everyday prison life, and most of all trying to stay alive in the process.

"Damn, the feds will hide a nigga"... The twenty-five years that he'd recently given back could attest to that. All his life Hakeem had been raised around triple O.G gangstas, who were bred, born, and raised by the code of the streets. All his life Hakeem had been taught to despise the very the very thing he'd been labeled...A notorious snitch nigga.

But the generational curse of a man standing strong, doing his time, and keeping his mouth shut had become a thing of the past. All the standup niggas were either dead or in prison doing sentences so long that their kid's kids, had kids. Times changed with the new generation and some of the most violent and notorious hustlers would flip before they could be driven down to the station. After returning to the streets, in most cases the very one they'd left. Other hustlers welcomed them back with open arms, instead of slaughtering them on the spot.

"Would you like a nice and naughty lap dance?" a short and thick redbone asked, breaking into his thoughts. Hakeem looked at his expensive watch once more. He had twenty more minutes before his two partners would be there, and hell they would probably be another half hour late anyway he figured.

'What da hell." He reached inside his Rock Ritual jeans and brought out a neat stack of large bills. That move alone caused the sexy stripper to begin moving gracefully around his chair in a sultry and seductive dance. She then raised her right leg and stepped over his lap and sat her damn near perfect ass down on his dick, which was already straining at his zipper. She grind, bounced and rotated that ass like her life was dependant on it.

"Man, how did you pull that off?" Jonathan asked his best friend Kevin's cousin who went by the name A.J.

"That shit was nothing kid; I do it all the time." He looked over at Jonathan, and then burst out into laughter.

"Whatchu laughing at?" Jonathan asked.

"You!"

"Me? Why the hell are you laughing at me?"

"Cause, nigga you still a virgin, that's why."

"What the hell you mean, I'm still a virgin, nigga I..."

"Chill, chill with the sensitive shit Jonathan, I'm not talking bout that type of virgin shit, I'm talking bout you never been inside a strip club homie."

"No I haven't, but what's the point?".

"There is no point, I just wanna give you the in's and out's with dis shit. And please don't sleep on these dancers bro… they got more game than half the niggas in this bitch."

"And?" Jonathan asked confused.

"And, nigga just keep a check on your pockets while they grinding on you. Oh yea also make sure you keep up with the song count. Because the DJ will put a mix on you and the chick will be talking threw the switch and the next thing you know you owe them for five songs and you won't remember one!" all of them started laughing.

"Gotcha."

"Good…now let's go feast on some ass and titties."

"Bout time you niggas showed up!" Hakeem said to the two young men dressed in matching red shirts and hats.

Without answering him they both immediately began throwing up several gang signs with their hands. Hakeem quickly answered with his own. As all three then burst out into yells.

"What up my nigga!!!!!!"

"Damn you two niggas ain't changed!" Hakeem shouted over the music.

"I see you haven't either," the bigger of the two said as he eyed the sexy stripper, making her way back towards the bar.

"Bitches, money and poppin bottles, will always be this nigga motto." Hakeem said describing himself.

"Fo sho." The smallest of the trio agreed.

"Speaking of money…What you got in mind on how the three of us gon eat my nigga?"

"Relax Lil Flo… in a few days money will be the least of our worries homie." He continued.

"But tonight it's all about poppin bottles, that kush, and these bitches."

"Speaking of bitches, I saw that broad you used to fuck wit earlier today." Lil Flo said.

"What broad?" Hakeem asked.

"I'm talking bout that caked up broad Keem… the one that's got damn near all of the queen city on lock."

"What's her name, Brianna or somethin like that?"

"Yea, yea that's that bitch name." Hakeem said.

"That bitch's neck and wrist was glaciered the fuck up… and that bitch was pushing a cocaine white Range Rover."

Hakeem didn't respond to Lil Flo's last statement, instead his mind momentarily wandered to Brianna. Damn, but he did miss that sweet tasting pussy she had between those long muscular legs, he thought. And her head game was nothing less than porn ready. He continued thinking… but that bitch had to pay for what she'd done to him. And she would. With her life, and some of that big bank she had.

"Yo Hakeem?" Lil Flo said interrupting his thoughts.

"Yea, what up Flo?"

"Yo, isn't that, that broad's little brother standing over there with them two young niggas?"

Hakeem focused his attention on the small group. And sure enough there standing inside the club was Brianna's younger brother. Hakeem smiled while thinking maybe, just maybe, He could give that dirty bitch something to think about.

Meanwhile Jonathan and his friends were enjoying the company of three strippers, when he stood up to leave.

"Where you going Jonathan?" Kevin asked.

Jonathan held up the empty bottle and then pointed towards the bar. Kevin smiled and then said, "Bring two."

"Alright." Then he disappeared through the thick crowd.

Jonathan was making his way back to the table when someone bumped into him, causing him to drop one of the bottles.

"Watch where the fuck you going nigga."

"You bumped into me." Jonathan shouted back at him.

Without another word the shorter man attacked him. Caught off guard with his hands full, Jonathan lost his balance and fell. But before the man could pounce on top of him, Jonathan rolled out the way and got back on his feet. Angry from being sucker punched he took the fight with the much shorter man, knocking him down,

Jonathan got on top of him and began working the smaller man over with rights and lefts. Just when he was about to finish it off, hands grabbed him from two different sides.

"Let me go! Let me the fuck go!"

"Chill Jonathan, chill out homie."It was Kevin and A.J. on his left. But it was the big bouncer guy on his right that held him with a vise like grip.

"Time for you little niggas to go." He growled.

"That nigga hit me first." Jonathan said, still angry.

"Don't matter, you three mother fuckers got to go."

The big bouncer marched all three of them to the front entrance of the club.

"Now get tha..." Jonathan started.

"Look out, he's got a gun!!!" someone yelled standing on the outside of the club. Gunfire erupted in front of them and the big man was forced to take a direct hit. He never saw it coming. Once he'd fallen to the ground Jonathan took the next heavy caliber slug to the chest.

"Jonathan!" his partner screamed.

"Somebody help us, please, somebody help! "Lay still Jonathan... just sit still... Don't try to move. Jonathan's other friend uttered.

"Look out!" somebody yelled again causing Jonathan's friend Kevin to look around in time to see Hakeem pointing a gun out the passenger's window of a car as it drove by. He seemed to be smiling over what had just happened. Off in the distance sirens could be heard. All Kevin could do was pray that they made it in time for his friend.

Chapter 10

Brianna kept her cool on the drive home from her date with Brandon. The last thing she wanted to do was to let him know the kind of insane tragedy that seemed to always happen in her life. He was the only pocket of the normal in her life, and ruining that was not an option.

As soon as he parked, she turned and gave him a kiss on the lips and rushed out of the car, not giving him the chance to open her car door.

Brandon, opened his door and yelled behind her, "You know that's now how I roll!"

"I know," she said over her shoulder, "I had a great time and I can't wait to do it again. But," she shrugged, "If I don't get inside quick, I might do something I'll regret later."

Brandon held out his hands in confusion, "What's that something?"

"Maybe you'll find out if you keep passing these tests!"

Before Brandon could say goodbye Brianna was inside the house kicking off her shoes and dialing Charrise's number.

"What hospital are you at?" she spat into the phone.

"Why the fuck weren't you answering your phone?" Charrise yelled.

"Don't make me ask you again! "

"CMC Main. Hurry up!"

Brianna quickly put on sneakers and rushed into the garage while still on the phone with Charrise.

"What happened!" For the first time since she'd seen the messages on her phone tears began to stream down her face.

"It's hard to says sis," Charrise said, "All I know is that he went out with his friends tonight and ended up getting shot. They called me as soon as they got to the emergency room."

"Nobody knows who did it?" Brianna said as she sped towards the highway.

"They don't, but I have an idea."

"Who?" Brianna shouted.

"Have you heard that Hakeem got out of prison?"

Brianna couldn't believe her ears. She felt the sickness bubbling in her stomach

"Yea Kasy mentioned something about it, but I didn't think it could be true."

"Yea Sis I'm here....... look I'm almost there, have they placed him in a room yet?"

"No not yet but....."

Brianna cut her off, "Have you called Kacy and Selena. They need find out who did this before the police do. And make sure you let Jonathan's friends no not to tell the police more than they tell us. Let'em know we will handle this in house, ok?"

"Aiight, I got'chu."

Brianna hung up the phone and looked up at the street sign to check her location. It read Kenilworth Ave. She was less than five minutes away from the hospital. She checked her rearview mirror, the light blue swirling lights made her pupils dilated immensely. For the first time Brianna recognized the sound of the sirens she could scarcely hear threw the silent confines of the luxury SUV. She quickly checked the speed gage she was only traveling five miles over the limit. So she figured she was not who the lights and sirens were meant for. Brianne slowly took her foot off the accelerator, clicked on the turn signal, and moved into the far right hand lane. She was trying to allow the cop car to go by her. To her disappointment he didn't pass her, instead he followed Brianne's vehicle into the lane. Damn she thought to herself she was just about to turn into the entrance to the emergency room. She went ahead and pulled her truck to a stop. The cop car did the same. It was confirmed now, because the officer was now exiting his cruiser and walking up to the driver side of the SUV. Brianne rolled down her window, just as he approached her door.

"License and registration please ma'am," the officer said in a long southern drawl.

"Did I do something wrong Sir?" Brianna asked in a low tone.

"License and registration." the Cop repeated, this time he shinned his heavy duty black flash light into Brianna's face, then directed it, into the area of her glove department.

Brianna did as she was told and retrieved the requested documents. As she placed them in his palm, she decided to make him aware of the crisis at hand.

"Sir I am really in a hurry, I have a family member who was rushed to the hospital."

"So is that why you where speeding and driving so recklessly this evening, Ms. Campbell?" the officer asked while looking at Brianne's license.

"Well sir I don't believe I was doing ether, but I don't have time for this, so could you please just write me the ticket so I can get to the emergency room?" This time she had taken the low tone out her voice and was visibly letting him know that she was pissed.

"You just sit tight and I will get you on your way, as soon as possible."

Brianna could tell in the officer's voice that she had aggravated him and he was going to show her who certainly had the authority. The cop took his time walking back to his patrol car. For no other reason except to further agitate Brianna he turned on his side door strobe light and shined it directly into her automobile.

After about 10 minutes, which seemed like 10 hours, the officer returned to the driver's side door.

"Ms. Campbell, we have a serious problem, it seems that you are wanted for questioning. The FBI has issued a warrant out for you, in association with an assault with intent to kill."

"A what?" Brianna played it off like she was unaware of their interest in her. "Officer I don't know anything about any warrant."

"I understand that, but I hope you understand that I am going to have to…"

"But what about my brother officer… can't this wait until I can at least find out if he is gonna live or die?"

"Please step out of the car ma'am." The officer said firmly.

"No officer, I will not step out of the car." Brianna said matching his tone evenly.

The officer stepped back and placed his hand upon the butt of his weapon.

"Ms. Campbell, I'm giving you a direct order to step out and away from the vehicle."

"And I said I will not step out or leave my car on the side of the highway. I know my rights, and as you stated I'm only wanted for questioning, not any type of actual crime officer, now I will be more than happy to be escorted down to the station." Brianna said looking him directly in his eyes.

The officer looked into her face and could tell she meant every word, he simply nodded his head slowly.

"Alright Ms. Campbell…I will follow you down to the station, but if you try anything I will personally put you and this car against the closest guard rail.

Brianna sat in the large room marked Interrogation on the door. There were pictures all around the room hanging on the wall. Some were Polaroid's, but most look like a professional photographers had taken them. The only thing different about the photo's was that none of the people in them was posing. Instead, the people in the images looked like they were not even aware that the images were being captured.

Brianna's thought's where interrupted by the older gray headed gentlemen that reminded her of her old junior high school principle.

"Hi Ms. Campbell, I'm agent Douglas with the FBI and this is my partner agent Garrard."

Brianna observed the much younger female agent that accompanied agent Douglas.

"Ms. Campbell do you know why we brought you here this evening?" The female agent asked

"No I'm not sure why, but let me correct one thing, I brought myself here tonight, thank you."

"Yes, I understand that, and we are hoping you can assist us with an open missing person case and possible homicide." Agent Garrard said, while placing a photo mug shoot on the table in front of Brianna.

Brianna looked down at the picture and her heart almost dropped out her chest. She tried to hold a stern face and act like she didn't know the man on the photo, but by the look on the agents' faces, it was too late. They could see that she knew exactly who Dre was. Rather than trying to convince them otherwise Brianna finally spoke.

"Yea I know him. He attended my sister's birthday party last year, is he in some type of trouble?" Brianna asked with a concern look on her face.

"Well yea I guess you can say that, Mr. Williams is missing and believed to be dead. The older agent chimed in.

"Now why would you guys think he's dead, He looks to be a grown man, so I'm pretty sure he could travel or relocate if he desired." Brianna stated nonchalantly.

"Ms. Campbell, we don't have you here to play games! Now we have a statement from a reliable source that states that you and Mr. Williams had a disagreement on the night of his disappearance. That same source has also confirmed that you and the alleged victim had business dealings and before you continue with these same shenanigans, know that we know what type of business you are currently involved in."

"And what type of business would that be, are you speaking of my investment company? Because if so I'm pretty sure when my lawyer arrives he will be more than happy to fill you in on our last year tax returns. And I'm positive that Mr. Williams was not involved in any of those investments." Brianna sat back in the chair satisfied with her answer.

The Older agent smiled and just has the younger female was about to contend with Brianna's rebuttal. Her attorney Mr. Consuelo walked in. Brianna was glad she had thought to call him while on her way to the station. He had arrived just in time, to save her before she ran out of answers for their questions.

"John it's great to see you again," Attorney Casteno spoke to the older agent as they shook hands.

He turned and looked at Agent Garrard, "Now this must be the new young agent that everyone is talking about. Well John you might want to let her know that's it's not a good idea to question a client, especially one of mine, without their lawyer present. And on that note, this interview is over." Attorney Casteno grabbed Brianna by her arm and lifted her out the small metal chair. He motioned for her to exit out of the hard iron door that he had just come through. Before fully shutting the door, he turned and yelled, "John we still on for our Saturday morning golf game? You know the Tee time is 8:00am."

Agent Douglas simply nodded his head in confirmation.

Chapter 11

Brianna pushed the button for a ticket as she entered the parking deck at CMC Main. She could barely remember her trek from the Police Department to the hospital. Her mind had been flooded with glimpses from the evening's events. As she led her car around the curves of the deck in search of a parking space her fingers were wrapped tightly around the steering wheel. Once she found a slot to drive into she put the car in park and released the wheel for the first time since she'd gotten inside. Her hands and fingers felt stiff and resisted her efforts to stretch them straight. She held them in front of her face and persisted with stretching, noticing the vibration that had taken over her. Brianna inhaled deeply, and held back tears.

'Damn B!' She told herself, 'You're supposed to be one of the baddest bitches in the city and you're getting shaken up by a little confrontation with the feds.' But she knew that it wasn't just the confrontation that had her shaken, it was the fact that her baby brother had received three bullets to his body.

The information Brianna knew had come from short cryptic emails from Charrise. Every time she thought of her Jonathan she couldn't help but see visions of Tre being assassinated right before her eyes. Sometimes it was Tre's face that she saw, other times it was Jonathan. Brianna took another moment to compose herself before exiting the car and heading into the hospital. She took the elevator down to the ground floor and entered into the lobby of the hotel to check in. After handing over her id and providing her brothers information, she was handed a visitors badge and directed to the elevators.

As she approached the elevator doors, she could see a blurry reflection of herself. Even with the blur she could tell she looked a mess. While waiting on the elevator Brianna corrected her messy ponytail by making a brush with her fingers. She scrambled inside of her purse to find lip gloss which she applied just as the elevator doors opened.

Jonathan's hospital floor was quiet and the lights were dim except for the nurse's station. As Brianna neared her brothers room she'd expected to hear voices and mumbles, but instead she heard more silence.

As she entered the room, all eyes immediately fell on her. All except Jonathan's who was asleep. Her mom, sister and Herman sat perched around his bed. She could easily tell that they'd all been crying from the puffy eyes and smeared makeup. That was everyone, except for Herman. Herman faced her with the same mean grimace that she'd always remembered him having. For a moment she paused to consider if she'd remembered ever seeing Herman smile. Not smirk, or pretend, but she searched her memory for a moment that she'd witnessed a true moment of happiness from the only father figure she'd ever known. Then the smiles from Herman appeared. But she noted that any true smile she'd ever witnessed had not ever been directed at her, or her mother for that matter.

Instead those moments of true happiness had been saved for his two blood children. As she stood in the doorway, she could feel his eyes scaling every inch of her being with a level of hate greater than he'd ever directed at her. A horrible feeling wrapped around her at trapped her inside a tight bubble. As Brianna attempted to move forward into the room the bubble stiffened around her making her immobile.

Herman took this opportunity to make an already glum Brianna, even more sullen. He shook his head, as if disappointed that she'd shown up.

"You know what Brianna," he started, "I knew you were a mistake from the moment I laid eyes on you. And when I realized that none of my blood was running through your veins, it all made sense. I wish… that we'da gotten rid of you then. But your trifflin' ass mother wouldn't let me. And this," he said while pointing at Jonathan," is the result. This is your fault. You do know that right?"

Brianna continued to stand in the doorway, not sure of what to do or what to say. She glanced over to her mother, and then to her sister, waiting for one of them to stand up for her. Neither of them said a word, still in shock from the night's events. She could tell in their eyes and faces that they didn't have the energy to fight with him, not even for her. Brianna knew, that they were saving every ounce of vitality they had left to pray and nurture Jonathan. She couldn't fault them for that.

The last thing Brianna wanted to do in that moment was to argue with Herman. She wanted to join forces with her mother and sister to help her little brother. She didn't want to encourage or add to the negativity that Herman carried with him everywhere he'd ever gone. But she also knew that she had to stand up for herself.

Brianna shook her head from left to right, "I'm not going to let you blame me for this Herman. We should be blaming whoever the knuckle head is who shot him!"

"What'chu mean you're not going to let me?" He laughed, "I already have! You're letting your brother die, just like you're letting me die! You think I don't know what the fuck is going on! I'm fucking dying and you won't let Charrise give us a penny! Now here Jonathan is lying in a hospital bed and I KNOW this has something to do with you! I can trace back every negative thing that's happened to our family to you!"

Finally Lorraine touched Herman's hand a quietly said, "Not now Herman... not now."

Herman quickly jerked his body away. He stood up, walking towards Brianna, "Don't tell me what to do!"

As he got closer to Brianna she could smell the liquor seeping from his skin. "Charrise is grown. She can do whatever the hell she wants to do with her money. But I don't blame her for not giving it to you. I can smell the alcohol on you now. Your ass can't stay sober even when you're dying from the very thing that you refuse to stay away from. You're a fucking joke! When I was a kid, I'd let all the negative stuff you said get into my head. But seriously Herman I couldn't care less about the drunken gibberish you let fall out of your mouth!"

By the time Brianna uttered her last word Herman was towering over her so close that their body's almost touched. He looked down at her with his signature grimace, "You think I'm a joke? We'll you're going to see how much of a joke I am when I head down to CMPD and tell them all of your little secrets."

Brianna stepped backwards into the hallway. "You'll probably die of alcohol poisoning or cirrhosis of the liver before you can make it there." She said shaking her head. "You don't scare me old man." Brianna said before turning and walking away. She simply refused to let him see her rattled. She couldn't help but question if Jonathan's shooting was in some way related to her. And after her meeting with the Feds, she considered the potential damage Herman could do if he actually did make it down to the Police Department to tell them anything. She was sure that Herman didn't really know what she and Charrise did for a living, but she also didn't need any additional attention to be brought her way.

Back inside the elevator Brianna couldn't hold her tears in any longer. They poured from her eyes like Niagara Falls.

Brianna pulled up to her home and got out of the car looking and feeling defeated. As she approached her door she heard the thump of running foot steps behind her. She turned around and noticed that Brandon was running up the block. He was wearing dark gray Nike gym shorts and a white tee-shirt. He hadn't spotted Brianna, but she still instinctively smoothed down her hair and brushed the wrinkles out of her clothes just before their eyes met.

Brianna had almost expected him to ignore her and turn the other way after the way she'd rushed away from him the night before with no explanation. Instead, he smiled, slowed his pace and came towards her.

"Good Morning." He said as he stopped short at the edge of her drive way.

Brianna walked to him and said, "Hello." Her eyes darted to the ground, embarrassed that she was still wearing the same clothes from their date.

"Is everything alright?"

Brianna looked up at him and shook her head no. She could see the surprise in his eyes as he noticed her bloodshot red eyes.

"I'm so sorry I rushed away last night," she started.

Brandon interrupted, "its ok, you don't have to explain."

"My brother got in a horrible accident," She continued, ignoring his comment. She needed to get it out by talking to someone about what she'd just gone through. Brandon wasn't her first choice, but he was definitely her first option. With Charrise still at the hospital and Selena on the prowl with Kacy trying to identify suspects, the last thing Brianna wanted to be was home alone.

Brandon intuitively wrapped his arms around Brianna, and she didn't hesitate to collapse into his sweaty embrace. "On top of that, I just got into a huge fight with my step-dad." Brianna began to cry all over again.

Brandon rubbed her back gently, "Do you want to go inside and talk?"

Brianna nodded and led the way inside her home. She collapsed onto the sofa finally realizing how exhausted she was. All night she'd allowed all of her emotions to take her body into auto pilot. Brianna told Brandon about her night, changing a few not-so-minor details. Rather than revealing that her brother hand been shot, she said he got into a car accident. She told him that she'd been stopped for speeding, and since she'd been going nearly 30 miles over the speed limit they took her in. She explained that after having her attorney meet her at the jail, she was released and went directly to the hospital where she'd argued with Herman.

"Damn," he mumbled, "That's a lot to go through in a night. You must be physically and emotionally exhausted."

"You have no idea." Brianna said.

"If you want, I'll stay here with you while you sleep." He said noticing the bags under Brianna's eyes.

"Will you lay with me," she asked in a child-like voice?

"I'd love to," he said, "but I'm all sweaty from running."

"Please," she said, "I need someone to hold me. You can take a shower here. My brother probably has some clothes here you can change into."

Even though Brandon only lived a block away, he was hesitant to leave Brianna in such a fragile state so he agreed to stay. In the master suite he helped Brianna undress and helped her into the shower. Just as he turned to leave she grabbed him by the arm and began to lift his shirt off, then his shorts and boxers, until nothing was left. Brianna pulled him into the shower with her and handed him her sponge and body wash, "Do you mind?" she asked?

"Not at all," Brandon said smoothly, attempting to hide his delight.

The walk in shower was tiled with small mosaic tile in varying shades of turquoise with a bench mounted in the corner. As the warm water sprayed over the pair Brandon busied himself adding body wash to the sponge and creating a foaming lather. Meanwhile Brianna bit her bottom lip as she intently gazed at his muscular body. Each muscle protrusion glistened as the water trickled over him. She was starting to feel a little better already.

He began at her neck and washed her body all the way to her toes, paying close attention to her breast and in between her thighs. Brianna's body burned with wanting as he grazed her nipples and clitoris. Brandon took the showerhead down from its perch and rinsed away all of the suds.

"Your turn," Brianna said taking the sponge into her hand. Brandon turned around and allowed Brianna to scrub his back and shoulders, when he turned around, his penis stood at attention. Without hesitation he effortlessly lifted up onto his shoulders taking her clitoris into his mouth. He sucked and licked rapidly making Brianna moan a squeal with delight. Brianna braced herself by wrapping her legs tightly around his neck and holding on to the back of his head. She grinded her torso in circular motions against his face needing to feel every swipe of his tongue. Her body had missed this feeling of euphoria and exploded with orgasm in a matter of seconds.

Once Brandon put her back down, she sat him down on the shower seat and straddled him backwards slowly inserting his penis into her warm wet pussy. She bounced up and down to the beat of the African drum that played in her mind. Pulsating to the rhythmic beat, first fast, then slow and then all over again and again until they both came in unison.

Both Brianna and Brandon panted heavily as they did their

best to catch their breath. Minutes later the pair were dried off and drifting off to sleep in bed spooning like old time lovers.

Charrise had finally given up her perch stance at the side of Jonathan's hospital bed. She had been determined not to leave his side until he woke up for the first time. She wanted her face to be one of the first, if not the very first face that he saw. Their parents had left shortly after Herman's argument with Brianna. As soon as she'd left Herman began to pace the floor spewing comments about his hatred for the step-daughter he never wanted. He seemed angry about everything, and his focus and concern about Jonathan had completely vanished. The more Lorraine asked him to calm down, the more riled up he became. Charrise sat there refusing to speak to either one of them. She could not put into words how ridiculous her father had become. Herman had once been the man that she looked up to and loved unconditionally. But as the years passed and he continued to sour, she could barely stand to be around him. After several minutes of her parent's non-stop quarreling, Lorraine announced that they were leaving. That had been the first thing Herman didn't object too. He hustled out of the door continue to mumble and murmur unintelligible sentences.

When Charisses' back couldn't take it anymore of her curved stance, one the nurses was kind enough to pull out the extra blankets and pillows so she could lie down on the day bed next to the window. Charrise quickly fell into a deep sleep. Hours later Charrise woke up to her brother's whispering voice.

"Sis," he said.

Charrise stirred a bit on the day bed before opening her eyes. As soon as she did, and noticed that her brother was finally awake, she hopped up with a massive smile.

"Oh my God! I was sooooo worried about you!" she said while rushing to his bedside. "How do you feel?"

"Terrible," he said, "I did get shot ya know," he said with a grin.

Charisse balled up her fist to deliver a playful punch, but stopped short of his shoulder. "Ooops, I guess I shouldn't be doing that."

"No, you shouldn't." He said, "You can't beat me up like you used too."

Charisse gave Jonathan the side-eye, "Not yet. I have faith that you'll make a full recovery. And when you do…"

"When I do what?"

"It'll be business as usual little bro." She said with a smile.

Nurses came to the room to check on Jonathan's pain level and .

Once Jonathan was fed and comfortable, Charrise resumed her perch on at the side of his bed.

"Where is everybody?" Jonathan asked, finally noticing that the rest of his family was absent.

Charrise sighed, "Everyone was here at one point or another. Butttttt, you know how it goes when we're all together. Daddy was drunk, he went off on Brianna telling her this was all her fault and…"

"Her fault," Jonathan asked with confusion coating his face, "How would this be her fault?"

Charrise shrugged, "Let daddy tell it, Brianna is the source of every negative thing that has ever happened to this family."

"He said that to her?"

"Yup," Charrise responded.

"Well I know for a fact this wasn't her fault. I was just in the wrong place at the wrong time… with the wrong crowd."

"Why you say that?"

"Cause we had to use fake id's and pay off the bouncer to get in the club at all. That should have been my first sign to turn around a leave."

"What the hell happened?'

"I guess the dude was just looking for a fight. The club was crowed and we bumped into each other. Dude got all out of his skin about it and the next thing I know we were on the floor brawling."

"So where'd the gun come into play?"

"Even though I didn't start the fight, the bouncers still threw me out cause we weren't really supposed to be in there. On the way out, I just remember somebody screaming then feeling this sharp pain in my shoulder and my arm. When I looked down and saw all that blood, I just blacked out."

Charrise's eyes welled up with tears as she envisioned her little brother being shot.

Jonathan placed his hand on Charrise's shoulder, "Don't cry Sis. I'ma be alright."

"Did you even know the guy?"

"Naw. Had never even seen him before." Jonathan shrugged and quickly winced with pain.

"Do you at least remember what he looked like?"

"He was short… dark skinned, and had long dreads."

Charrise froze envisioning Hakeem in her mind. Sure, the physical description matched, but what matched even more was the reckless way the shooter had aimed and fired through a crowd full of people. Jonathan had never met Hakeem directly, but they'd certainly crossed paths once or twice because their connections to Brianna. Enough times for Hakeem to be able to identify him as Brianna's brother.

Before Charrise could respond, Jonathan's friends, A.J. and Kevin, appeared in the doorway. The pair looked almost afraid to enter. They looked younger than Charrise had remembered. She couldn't help but wonder what type of security guard would let these guys into a club. It was one of those instances in life where everyone thought of the what ifs and maybes. What if the security guard would have turned them around at the door? Maybe her brother wouldn't lying here in a hospital bed. After all, it was his job to make sure the club was secure, and letting three knuckle heads in certainly should have been against his better judgment. Charrise's mind was locked in a circle of thoughts when Jonathan snapped her out of it.

"Sup niggas!" Jonathan yelled from the bed, "y'all coming in or not."

Their eyes simultaneously darted towards Charrise, who nodded with approval. She didn't blame them. Instead a steady rage was building up in her for Hakeem. Blaming the security guard was pointless. There was no way he could have predicted how the night would end. The blame lay solely on Hakeem. Tracing everything back to the beginning, he had been the true source of negativity.

One could attempt to blame Brianna for this because she'd been the one to get Hakeem caught up and arrested. But she would have never even known Hakeem if it wasn't for Tre. And Tre certainly couldn't be blamed considering the fact that Hakeem had murdered him. Putting him behind bars had only stopped him temporarily. In that moment Charisse fully understood the importance of getting rid of Hakeem.

With Jonathan's friends visiting, Charisse felt comfortable heading home. She walked over to kiss him on the forehead before heading out. "Aiight, I'm leaving. I'll let mom and dad know that you're up so they'll probably be by pretty soon. I can come back and spend the night here with you again if you want."

"Ok, I'll let you know." Jonathan replied.

Charisse waved goodbye to Jonathan and his friends as she exited the hospital room.

Charisse dropped her keys on the console in the front hallway as she walked in the house. Ahead of her she could see the directly into the living room where the TV had been mounted above the fire place. Selena lay curled up on the sofa with her cellphone positioned between her shoulder and ear. She had a smile on her face that was wider and shinning more so than Charisse had ever witnessed on Selena's face. Charisse stood, unnoticed, hovering over Selena for a few minutes before Selena broke out into laughter and turned on her back. Her mouth gapped open with surprise when she finally noticed that she was being watched.

"Hold on a minute, babe." Selena said into the receiver.

"Babe?" Charisse asked in shock.

Selena narrowed her eyes and cupped her hand over the phone, "Don't be a hater," she said with a grin, "Now what's up?"

"Where's B? I need to have a word with both of ya'll."

Selena simply pointed upstairs and returned to her conversation. Charisse rolled her eyes and headed in the direction of Brianna's room. When Charisse opened the bedroom door she counted four bare feet peaking form underneath the covers on the bed. Charisse rubbed her eyes, figuring that her lack of sleep was making her see doubles. But she looked again; there was no denying that there was an extra pair of feet hanging from her sister's bed.

Her lips morphed into a jealous scowl. It was not lost on her that while she was up all night watching over her brother, Selena and Brianna had been up all night with men that were not blood related to her. Charisse's mind quickly drifted to some of her better memories of her relationship with Dre. She stood in Brianna's doorway in a reflective daze remembering what it felt like to be wrapped in the warm arms of a man. Charrise had been on a constant hunt to find a male companion, but every time she got close, she'd have flash backs of getting beaten. Those memories constantly stopped her in her tracks. She'd wrecked her brain trying to figure out what signs Dre had exhibited that she's simply ignored. But she couldn't put her finger on anything specifically. She'd chalked up his possessive and jealous ways of manhood. After all, she'd dated guys in the past that had those qualities, but none that ever dared to put their hands on her. As much as Charrise wanted a man, she knew that she'd never let anyone get that close to her until she uncovered the mystery that kept plaguing her thoughts.

When the covers on Brianna's bed began to move, Charrise snapped out of her deep thoughts and loudly cleared her throat.

Brianna and Brandon's head quickly and simultaneously popped up from underneath the sheets. They looked at Charrise and then at each other. Grins crept onto their faces as they remembered what actions had brought them to this very moment.

"Uuuuhhhhh… you remember…" Brianna started.

Charrise interrupted her swiftly saying, "Yeah, I remember. No introduction needed. Sorry to break up the party but, I need to see you once your company leaves."

Brianna's grin quickly turned into a worried grimace as she wondered what Charisse had to thell her.

She abruptly turned around and slammed the door behind her. Charrise entered the living room just as Selena was hanging up the phone with her new boo. That familiar jealous scowl reappeared on Charisse's face as she plopped down in the middle of the sofa.

"What's that face for?" Selena asked? "Let me find out somebody's jealous!"

Charrise ignored the statement and snatched the remote control from Selena's hand. She busied herself flipping through channels while she anxiously waited for Brianna to emerge from her room.

Nearly ten minutes passed before Selena and Charrise heard shuffling towards the front door followed by the sounds of the closing door and locks turning. Brianna made her way into the living room and settled in on the opposite side of the sofa opposite

Selena creating a Charrise sandwich.

"What are you sitting here pouting about?" Brianna asked her sister.

Before Charrise had a chance to say anything Selena jumped in, "I think she's jealous cause everybody's booed up but her."

Brianna smirked, "You too?" she asked Selena.

"Yeah, I can't let you get all the action," she responded with a laugh.

"Ok, we need to get a double date on the calendar!"

Charrise exhaled loudly interrupting the conversation between Brianna and Selena. She had heard enough. If they were going to gloat about their love lives, Charrise didn't want to hear about it. At least not until she found a man for herself.

"Aiight... my bad. What's up?" Brianna asked.

"I think Hakeem shot Jonathan," Charrise blurted out completely changing the tone of the conversation. Negative energy seemed to cloud the room the moment Hakeem's name was uttered.

Brianna quickly sat upright, "Why you say that?"

Charrise shrugged, "I don't know for sure it was him... but the way Jonathan was describing the guy that shot him. I can't think of nobody else."

Selena chimed in, "Actually, that is the word on the street."

"You and Kacy went scouting for info?"

"Yeah, and all trails lead to Hakeem."

Brianna shook her head while she tried to wrap her mind around what the girls were saying. "What did Jonathan say?"

"He said that he had gone to the bar to get a drink and when he was walking back short guy with dreads bumped into him and made him drop his drink. He was like, even though the guy had bumped into him the guy was pissed about it. He said they exchanged a few words and the next thing he knew they were brawling. The bouncer came and scooped him up quick because they weren't supposed to even be in the club in the first place. Right when they got to the front of the club, he heard somebody yell gun right before he felt the bullet."

Brianna visualized the scene in her mind. The face and the stance of the shooter was Havok's . She had spared his life, even when he didn't have the decency to spare her own, or Tre's life, the man that had been closer to him than a brother. In that moment, she knew that she'd made a huge mistake in sending Hakeem to jail instead of to the grave.

"So Herman was right… if Hakeem did do this, it was my fault." Brianna said sinking back into the sofa with tears falling out of her eyes.

Charrise shook her head fiercely, "Don't say that!" she yelled.

"Why not," Brianna yelled back, "it's true isn't it?'

"No! It ain't nobody's fault but Hakeem! I'm not going to let you blame yourself for this B! That ain't right!"

"Whatever Charrise. I don't wanna sit here and argue the point with you."

Selena interjected, "Blame is beside the point. We need to figure out what we're going to do to alleviate the problem right now."

"What do you have in mind?" Brianna asked quickly.

"It seems to me like there's only one good option left."

Brianna and Charrise both nodded in agreement and understanding. It was just that simple, his life or theirs. He'd made that clear by shooting Jonathan. Brianna was not prepared to allow Hakeem the right to kill off all of the people who she was closest too. And although she wasn't thrilled about taking the life of any one, she wasn't against it in this case. As far as she was concerned, he had it coming, and she was the best woman for the job.

Just before Brianna got up and left she remembered what she'd forgotten to tell the girls.

"Ooooohhh yeah!" she said, "I didn't even get to tell ya'll about what happened to me on my way to the hospital."

Charrise nodded, "I was wondering what was taking you so long," she said remembering that she'd been watching the door for her sister's arrival the night Jonathan had been shot.

"I got pulled over for speeding and when they checked my id they told me I was wanted by the feds for questioning."

"The feds?" Selena said in shock.

"Yes girl! I was shook. I even thought about speeding off, but I knew that wasn't going to do me any good."

"What'd they want?"

Brianna exhaled loudly, "Girl where do I even begin with that. It's too much to even try to repeat right now, but now that I know that Hakeem is up to no go, it all makes sense. The only way he got out early was to snitch so ya'll know he told them about me."

Chapter 12

Herman & Hakeem:

After the leaving the hospital in the early crack of dawn of the new sunny day, Herman decided against sleeping in for the remainder of the morning. Instead he elected to jump in the shower and put on some clothes and head out. Loraine didn't think much of this. Lately, Herman's normal morning routine had consisted of him sleeping well until afternoon. Then he would get up and throw on some clothes, usually the same ones from the previous day, and walk up to the nearby corner store to purchase his morning medicine; which was any hard liquor that was the cheapest or on sale. As so long as it kept him drunk and numb to everything going on around him and inside himself, he was happy with the tonic.

The one thing that did draw a small level of suspicion was the fact that he had taken a shower this morning and had clean clothes laid out. It had been many years since Loraine had worried about her husband committing some form of adulterous acts. And truth be told, at this point she couldn't care less. In fact, if it would put her husband in a more pleasant mood, she would iron the clothes for him to go meet his potential extracurricular activity. Hell, she thought to herself, 'Lords knows I've thought about it lately'. It was not like they were being intimate, but deep down inside Loraine knew that was never Herman's personality. Her mind drifted back to its somber mood once she heard the door shut signaling that Herman had exited the house.

Once outside, Herman placed the car in neutral, so that he could crank it up. The fact that he had to go thru this every time he started his automobile made his blood boil. He could remember the days when he had only the best of everything, when small problems like this would lead him to purchase a brand new car. Instead here he was on what felt like the tenth turn of the key with hopes of the engine finally turning over. All this and the sweat building up on his forehead from the interior heat of the car reminded him of his step daughter and all the wealth she had decided to hold back from him and her own mother.

"Who do this little bitch think she is? And last night she had the nerve to talk back to me and make a loose threat! I'll show this little red nigga," he spoke to himself.

Finally he heard the roar of the engine. It only took him 30 minutes to arrive at his destination; 10 of which were used on him stopping to grab a bottle of Mad dog 20/20. Herman got out the car and stared at the old sign that had begun to pull away from the white brick building. He fumbled threw all of the keys that were attached to his belt key ring until he found the one for the door that lead inside of his very first and only current operating restaurant. It had been weeks since the last time he had it open for business and the smell that ran threw his nostrils upon opening the door was a grave reminder of that fact.

Herman made his way to the backroom and to the gray metal panel that controlled all the lights and electrical fryers. He moved each black switch from the off position to the opposite side. The whole place lit up and the sounds of the oldies but goodies radio station came blaring threw the old building.

"Something's going on some ones on the phone three o'clock in the morning talking about how she can make it right." Herman immediately began singing along and popping his fingers. "Man when this was out I know I was the shit!" he yelled out while thinking to himself about the good ole days once again. "Love and Happiness!" He screamed even louder, while walking back into the large freezer, where he grabbed some bags of freezer burnt fries and hamburger patties. Herman's restaurant sat on the corner of LaSalle and Beatties Ford Rd. where all the hustlers, thieves, and addicts went to exchange their goods. So even though the restaurant hadn't been open in a long time. It wouldn't matter once all the natives awoke and needed something good to eat. Herman had what was called the Poe Boy Special which consisted of a large patty burger with fries piled up on top and his signature secret sauce, which was nothing more than mayonnaise, ketchup, and barbeque sauce. But for the low price of $2.99 it was hard to beat especially since it came with a drink.

Several hours had passed and Herman was really feeling better about himself. He had already made close to $300.00 and it wasn't even 5:00pm.

He thought to himself. "Shit this ain't bad considering all I had was some old fries and burgers and a few can sodas."

His thoughts were interrupted by the jingle on the door chime, beckoning his attention towards another customer entering the small establishment. The dark long dread head man stood and looked over the inside of the place, like a potential buyer of the property. Herman and the potential customer locked eyes for what seemed like an hour before the young man spoke.

"Hey Ole head, you the owner?" the man asked nonchalantly. Herman wasn't sure how to respond.

Normally he would say no just in case it was a bill collector or worst someone from the city tax or health department. But based on the way the young man was dressed and all the jewelry hanging from his body Herman was sure that none of it could have been purchased on a government salary.

"Yea I'm the owner and who wants to know?" he asked with a defiant tone.

"Chill old man, I'm about to make your day, hell probably your year with what I need to talk to you about."

"O yea and what would that be" Herman asked with hesitance. "Let's just say you and I have two common enemies and one can help us remove the other."

"Huh?" Herman exclaimed with a look of curiosity, "I don't even know you, what possible enemies could we both have?"

The dread headed man simply smiled before he continued speaking. "Yea, like I said two common enemies, one is money or the lack of it and the second is your step daughter Brianna."

Herman's eyes lit up and his attention fixated on every word the young man spoke thereafter. "So why don't you make me and yourself one of those Poe Boy specials and come have a seat so we can discuss this further. Oh, and by the way, my name is Hakeem".

****

Brianna's heart was warmed when she noticed the bright smile on her brother's face as she entered the roundabout in front of Carolina's Medical Center main. She released a sigh of release, not only because he was alive, but also because it was clear that he wasn't blaming her for being shot.

She quickly parked and got out of the car. Jonathan was seated in a wheelchair with the hospital escort positioned behind him. Brianna walked to his side and leaned over to give him a hug. Jonathan winced with pain as his sister circled her arms around him.

Brianna quickly released him saying, "I'm sorry. I didn't mean to hurt you!"

"Chill sis," he said putting her nerves at ease. "If I can take a few bullets, I sure as hell can live through a hug from you."

With the help of the escort Brianna helped a weak Jonathan into the car.

No sooner that Brianna placed her bottom in the driver's seat she started in with questions, "How are you feeling? Has mom been back up here to visit? You're ok with staying with me and Charrise, right?" Brianna rattled off question after question in a rapid pace. There was so much she wanted to know.

"Do I need to tell you to chill again," he said laughing. "I ain't never seen you this nervous. Are you okay?"

"No. I'm your big sister and I'm worried. You can't fault me for that. I don't want anything bad to happen to you. "

"True, true. I'm actually happy that you're letting me stay with you. Charrise told me about what dad said to you when you tried to come visit me. I don't even want to see him right now. I can't believe he's trying to blame you for this."

Guilt started to creep into Brianna's heart as she listened to her brother. She knew that he didn't deserve to be going through this. She shook off the feelings of guilt, know that rather than blaming herself, she should be blaming the menace to society himself.

"I've got your room all set up so you can be comfortable." She said but what she was really thinking was that Jonathan was much safer in her home rather than in the home of her parents. At this point, she didn't quite know what to expect out of Hakeem. But she knew that if he would shoot her baby brother in front of hundreds of people at the club, it was just the start of his plot to revenge. It was clear to her that he had no limitations and it was time for her to work on a plan of her own to stop him in his tracks.

She kicked herself for not having him killed right along with Andre. He'd already left a whole in her heart by killing Tre, and it made her sick to her stomach to think that she could have lost Jonathan. Murder was the only way to deal with somebody like him. She knew that if she didn't kill him, he'd never stop trying bring her down.

Breaking away from her thoughts Brianna asked, "So what did mom and Herman say when you told them you were going to stay with me?"

"I didn't tell him yet." Jonathan responded.

"Ooooooo," Brianna teased, "You gone be in trouble!"

"Whatever! I'll call'em and tell him right now!"

Jonathan pulled out his cellphone and dialed his dad's number.

"Put him on speaker," Brianna suggested.

"Hello?" Herman's raspy voice came through the receiver.

"Hey Dad!"

"Hey J! When are they letting you outta that hospital?" Herman said sounding chipper.

"Actually they released me today."

"Ok, you shoulda said something! I'll be on my way to get you."

"No need," Jonathan told him, "Brianna picked me up."

"Oh," He said, his voice turning cold, "Well you might as well have her take you back. I don't want her around this house anymore."

Brianna shook her head in disgust and rolled her eyes. He had some nerve.

"Nah dad, I'm actually going to stay with her and Charrise."

"What that hell you mean you staying with Brianna and Charrise? Now, do like I told you to do and tell her to drop you back off! I'm coming to get you now!" Herman screamed.

"I meant what I said dad. I'm not moving back in over there."

"Now how are you going to turn your back on your sick dad?" Herman asked playing the guilt card. "We need you home!"

Jonathan didn't back down, "That's not your decision anymore dad. "

"What? Who do you think you're talking to like that?"

"Look," Jonathan shrugged, "I'll still come check on you. But it's time for me to move on."

Venom coated Herman's words as he continued to speak, "I hope you know that it's Brianna's fault you even got shot in the first place. I can't believe that little bitch is taking you too! We'll you know what fuck her and fu—"

Jonathan hung up before Herman could finish his sentence. He looked over at Brianna to see how she was taking the harsh words Herman had dished out. He put his hand on her shoulder, "You know..."

Brianna shook her head, "No need to make excuses for him lil bro. I'm used to it anyway."

Herman's word no longer affected Brianna the way they had when she was a child. After her last interaction with him it was clear that he was a bitter old man. And the fact that his health was steady declining with cirrhosis of the liver, Brianna couldn't be happier. She'd washed her hands of him knowing that he was digging his own grave.

Charrise greeted Brianna and Jonathan at the door of their home with open arms. She showed him to his room that had been redecorated in his favorite colors. His new bedframe was made of black leather tufted with large buttons. A plush solid red duvet set with fluffy pillows welcomed him as he laid his aching body onto the thick mattress.

Jonathan lay in the middle of the bed watching his new 60 inch flat screen TV with his two sisters flanking him.

"How are you feeling?" Charrise asked.

"Great. Ya'll are treating me like a king. I may never leave," he said grinning from ear to ear.

"Well sit up for a second so you can take these pain meds." Brianna instructed him as she passed him glass of water and two hydrocodone pills.

Jonathan did as he was told while his sisters watched over him lovingly until he drifted to sleep.

Brianna and Charrise tiptoed out of Jonathan's room headed towards the living room.

"Have you heard from Selena?" Brianna asked Charrise.

"She's booed up, as usual." Charrise responded.

"Ok, well I'ma text her cause we need to have another meeting tomorrow."

"Oh yeah, about what this time?"

"It's time to start plotting on Hakeem. We've done enough of talking about all the havoc he's causing in our lives and it's time we put him down for good."

"Aiight! You know I'm down. But why wait? We can probably get her to come over tonight… and Kacy too."

"Nah, it can wait till tomorrow. I got plans tonight any way."

Charrise looked at her sister knowingly, "What kinda plans?"

Brianna couldn't help the grin that automatically spread across her face, "let's just say that Selena ain't going to be the only one booed up tonight."

"Yeah, yeah. Go get you some." Charrise said trying not to be a hater, "I'll stay her and watch out for Jonathan. But tomorrow it's time to get to business."

"Yes ma'am." Brianna answered as she walked out the door. She headed down the block to spend the night with Brandon. She was starting to like him more and more.

****

Tank cruised through the dark streets of Charlotte with his always serious and to the point street mentor, Cowboy, riding shotgun. The gritty sounds of Yo Gotti reverberated from the old school Caprice Classic's sound system. Every so often Tank would check the time on his watch. Then without giving himself away he would periodically sneak a glance over at his passenger whose facial expression never seemed to change. His appearance seemed like that of a statue with eyes that blinked very little. It was as if his entire being lived in another place. Tank was in no way gay, but he instantly began thinking that Cowboy was probably a real ladies man in his day. Even though Cowboy was well into his mid to late 50's he was still what women would consider attractive. He had nice wavy hair and very strong facial features. His body was built like a 25 year old boxer that most likely came from long stenches in prison. The penitentiary had a way of preserving nigga's.

Tank made another right turn, in hopes of concealing the destination to Cowboy. Although he trusted the old man with his life, Tank understood the less his potential codefendant knew, the better it would be for all involved.

What Tank hadn't recognized was the fact that Cowboy was very aware his surroundings. In fact, his senses were so keened, focused and alert that he could easily recount the exact amount of times that Tank had checked and rechecked the timepiece on his arm. Cowboy, without the slightest hesitation, could just as easily slide over into the driver's seat, put the car in reverse and retrace the street they'd traveled on the past two hours. It wasn't until they had turned on a very familiar street that Cowboy finally broke his eerie silence.

"Where you going boy?" he asked Tank.

Before answering him Tank looked at his Benny watch again.

"Chill Unk, a couple more blocks and we'll be there."

Cowboy started to question Tank again, but quickly decided against it. Instead he settled himself back against the seat and willed himself to be quit as Tank killed the car headlights just before he pulled into a driveway that was all too familiar to him.

****

Charrise awoke to the sound of her latest ringtone. She grabbed her phone while trying to clear the sleep from her eyes. After focusing she looked down at the screen to see her mother's name appear.

"Oh God." She thought to herself. This was a call she had been both expecting and regretting at the same time.

She looked at the clock on the phone docking station and charger. It read 2:45 A.M. Charrise knew that a phone call from her mother at this hour was not good news. Hell if it was 2:45 in the afternoon, Loraine never called, except to complain or report bad news. But still she was her mom… Charrise continued thinking, and she loved her dearly.

"Yes mom, what is it?" Charrise answered.

"It's not your mother, this is your father." Herman whispered groggily into the receiver.

"Daddy, is everything okay, where is mommy?" Charisse responded, panic instantly took over her.

"That is why I'm calling you, me and your mother had a big argument and she stormed out the house about six hours ago."

"Where did she go daddy?"

"I'm not sure where she went but as you can see she left her phone, and I'm starting to get worried about her because she has never left the house for this long and not called..." he paused for a moment and then continued in his low raspy voice. "I was hoping you could come by and give me a lift up to the gambling store, that car of mine won't crank."

"Gambling store?" Charisse asked.

"Yes you know your mother liked to go up there and play the online slot machines, but that's not a place for women to be this time of night.

Herman could here Charisse fumbling with her phone.

"Are you still there? Hello?" he asked.

"I'm still here I just dropped my phone." She answered.

"Look, I'm on my way out the door now, I'll be there in twenty minutes."

"Okay, I'll be waiting," Herman answered.

After disconnecting with his daughter, Herman quickly began to dial another number.

He waited...

"Yo, what up?" Hakeem asked after answering the phone.

"Everything is a go." Herman said weakly.

"That's good old man that's real good; I'll make sure to relay that to my peoples, ya heard?"

What about the money?' Herman asked in a more determined voice this time.

"Easy pops I got ya bread right here, I'll give it to you as soon as the switch is done.

"And no one will be hurt right?"

"That's right old man... and before you ask your money will be in the exact place that we discussed it would be."

"If it's not in the exact place where we talked about Son I will have the whole Mecklenburg County police department swarming this city looking for you."

"Like I said, the money will be there, and don't be threating me with that cop shit, you sick motha fucka." Hakeem snapped back through the phone.

"Take it easy young buck, I –I just need that money is all." Herman said in a much more mellow tone of voice that time.

"Aight that sounds a lot better." Hakeem screamed

"Someone's pulling up in my driveway now is that your people?"

"No it must be her; you just sit tight and don't move until you hear my signal."

"Alright but remember what we agreed upon, don't hurt her!"

He had no idea that his request had fallen upon deaf ears. Hakeem had already hung up the phone and called Tank.

Charisse pulled into her parents drive way quickly bringing her baby blue Lexus to a stop.

"Why is it that every time I come over her, it's so dark, how many times do I have to remind them to keep the porch lights on?" she thought to herself while trying to buckle her Mark Jacob sandals onto her feet.

With her mind still transfixed on her parents lack of lighting Charisse didn't notice the two shady figures approaching her vehicle until it was too late. She jumped out the car and took about three steps when she walked into something that felt like a tree. The impact from the blow knocked her off balance and momentarily forced all of the air out of her lungs.

Just as she started to recover Charisse looked up at the looming dark figure, a figure she recognized was that of a man.

"Who the hell are you, and what are you doing wandering around my parent's house?" she struggled to get her words out her mouth.

The unknown figure didn't answer her, but instead he reached down and grabbed her by one of her wrist.

"Let me go!" Charisse immediately started to scream. "get off of me!" she yelled. She began kicking and swinging her one loose arm wildly. "Get off…" her words were cut off by a powerful hand that clamped over her mouth.

"Shut that bitch up Unk."She heard someone say behind her. With sheer fright taking over, Charisse fought with all the power her small body could muster.

"Hold that bitch still Unk."

"I got her boy…ouch!" he screamed.

"What Unk?"

"'This girl just bit me!" he shouted.

Tank grabbed her, "hold still bitch!"

"NO!" Charisse screamed.

Left with no choice Tank raised his pistol, and then brought the butt of his gun down against her head. The blow from the butt of the firearm hit the back of her head so hard, it sounded like a peach dropping onto the concrete. Her small body fell towards the ground, only to be grabbed and held up by Cowboy.

"Open the trunk boy."

"Why? Just put the bitch in the back seat Unk." Tank said.

Cowboy gave Tank a long hard stare before responding.

"Boy it's too risky to put her in back seat, do you want us to get life for kidnapping?"

"Hell no, you know better than that Unk."

"Well I suggest you open this damn trunk" Cowboy repeated as he carried Charisse's 120 pound limp body around to the back of the car.

After securing their target inside the trunk, Tank retrieved a brown paper bag from the front seat. He quickly ran over to the large patio of the home and tossed the bag up against the door. He then ran, jumped into the car, and sped off.

Chapter 13

Brianna came home with first thing in the morning after receiving a text from Charrise letting her know that she had gone to help out Herman with something. After checking in on Jonathan and giving him more meds, she sat alone inside a small section of her home that she'd turned into what she referred to as the "Sanctuary room." She had installed fish tanks in the wall and had the constant sounds of the water fall that refilled them automatically.

Sipping on a bottle of flavored Moscato, her mind drifted back to the events and meetings over the past two weeks. Her entire organization wanted revenge… and so did she.

Brianna knew that she would have to retaliate for what had happened to her brother. She also knew that vengeance would have to be brutal and unforgettable. In the underworld, problems with yo' street family was handled or resolved in the streets, but when it came to blood family, the message sent back to the adversaries involved could be nothing less than a toe tag. Brianna's expression turned into a vicious smile as she thought of Hakeem. She hated him more than anything on earth. Her thoughts turned to her last meeting with Kasy and Selena and the conversations that had proceeded.

"No Bri… Listen to me ma, we gots to find dis nigga right now and deal with this shit.. you feel me? If not every motha fucka in dis city gon come at us" Kasy said.

"Yea I feel you and I understand that Kasy but…"

"But what?" he yelled in frustration, he instantly tried to calm his tone and begun to speak softer.

"Look Bri, this nigga shot you baby brother down in cold blood right in front of four, five hundred people. And don't forget half them niggas was go hard street niggas just like you and me. What do you think those niggas is thinking right now? I'll tell you what they thinking, them niggas is already making plans to come at us Bri... we have got to show them motha fuckas we playing for keeps,"

Brianna sat quietly listened for a long time without saying anything. She knew that everything her most trusted soldier had said was true. There was no way she could allow an act like that to happen and not be handled. She could not allow something else to happen to her family.

"You right Kasy, we cannot let this shit just wash away. But this situation with the Feds has really got me shook right now. And I'm thinking we all need to lay low, because word on the street is that fucking with Hakeem is like fucking with the Feds since he's working with them. But a message must be sent to let everyone know, what happens when you fuck with me and mines. So let's touch the little niggas who was with him and that bitch of his who has had something coming to her trifling ass anyway. And we will save that bitch nigga for later." She said. She gave them both a sinister smile.

"That's what the fuck I'm talking bout murder mami." Selena shouted out from a quiet corner of the room. Brianna nodded her head in agreement, just as her phone rang. The small screen on the apple IPhone came to life with the name Baby-Sis and the option for facetime. Brianna quickly pressed accept and a very clear image of her baby sister Charisse bound by the hands and feet popped up. A large black male hand removed the gag that was stuffed in Charisse's mouth.

"Bri please help me. These men are going to kill me...please he....." before she could finish, the same large man forced the gag back in her mouth. He spoke into the phone with a clear deep voice.

"Listen up bitch, you've got 48 hours to come up with Three Hundred and fifty thousand. If not you can say goodbye to this lil sexy bitch of a sister of yours. And we'll be sure to enjoy every part of her before we put her to rest! And keep your phone near you because I will be calling you back with the details of where to bring that paper! You got that bitch?"

All Brianna could do was shake her head in agreement, as tears rolled down both of her cheeks. She quickly tried to wipe them away because she knew that it was not the time for weakness.

Charisse continued to scream at the phone in hopes that by some miracle Brianne could come rescue her instantly. But her pleas went unanswered, at least temporally.

"Look shorty, it's no need to do all that hollering, the phone has already hung up and it's no way anyone can hear you all the way out here. But if you just like something in your mouth, keep it up, because I got something perfect for it." Tank said while grabbing his dick.

The other men standing around him began to laugh. All except Cowboy, he stood there with his normal business face, before he motioned for Tank to follow him. Once outside the small house that sat on the North and South Carolina border town of Fort Mill. Cowboy spoke his peace with Tank.

"Look youngin if my work is done, I'd like to be compensated and I can leave you boys to you'll business." He uttered in a quite tone.

Tank looked down at his phone, as he contemplated calling Hakeem to see if Cowboy's services were still needed, but decided against it. He figured that he was second in charge and was more than capable of making the decision.

"Unk, you good for right now, but I can't break bread with you until this job is seen all the way through, you feel me?"

"Yea, I feel you youngin, but put something in my pocket until that time and have one of the young boys drop me off at the house and I'll catch up with you tomorrow."

Tank could sense that Cowboy was ready to leave, so he didn't put up a fight. Instead he hollered inside to one of the two men that were watching Charisse and instructed him to take Cowboy home and to come right back. Once he was back inside Tank and Duke popped open a small jug of syrup. Syrup was the new drink that was sweeping the south. All anyone needed was cough syrup, sprite, jolly ranchers, and some white Styrofoam cups and it was an instant party or sleep fest.

After a couple of swigs, Duke looked at Tank and asked, "So

what you think, you want to give shorty a sip?" He pointed over to Charisse.

"Do you think the little bitch can handle this shit?" Tank asked back.

"Bro you know them bitches go crazy on this shit, especially if it's her first time, you feel me?" Duke spoke with a sly look on his face.

"Nigga I feel you and I'm ahead of you, shit I think I got some bars in my car, we can mix the two and I know this bitch will get right!

"Hell yea my nigga grab them and let's get this party started right!" Duke screamed while giving Tank some dap.

Once Tank had come back in from retrieving the Xanax from the glove compartment of his car, he removed the gag from Charisse's mouth and placed the cup up to her lips, while Duke held her nose so she would have to swallow. Charisse did all she could to not allow the men to pour their concoction down her throat, but to no avail. No matter how much she shook her head back in forth. The majority of the drink, followed by the pills, flowed directly down her throat. Duke was right; it didn't take long for the drugs to begin to take effect on Charisse. She was completely out of it and singing along with the music video the men had blasted on the large plasma TV.

"I wear Gucci I wear Prata at the same damn time
On the phone cooking dope at the same damn time
Selling white selling mid at the same damn time
Fucking 2 bad bitches at the same damn time
At the same damn time, at the same damn time
At the same damn time, at the same damn time
I'm at Pluto I'm at Mars at the same damn time
On the sofa popping bottles at the same damn time"

"O yea that's what I'm talking about lil mama, Duke go ahead and un-tie her I think she ready to really party with some niggas, ain't that right Tank asked looking back at Charisse and smiling." Duke was well ahead of him and began removing the ties that was placed around Charisse's hands and feet. Charisse staggered up and began to dance to the music. She was all off beat, but it didn't seem to bother Tank or Duke. Both men were too busy removing her clothes, until she stood before them completely nude.

Tank quickly laid her back on the small oil stained sofa that sat in the old house. He took a complete look at Charisse, She was truly the most beautiful woman he had seen naked that wasn't shaking her ass and asking for him to make it rain. But even those women couldn't measure up to what was before him, he thought to himself, totally forgetting that Duke was even present. Tank parted Charisse's legs gently and began to feast on her insides. Something in the inside of Charisse told her to push him away. But the effects of the drugs had fully taken over her physically and instead she grabbed the back of his head and pulled him deeper into her womanhood.

Duke, seeing that Tank had claimed his spot, pulled out his long black dick and placed it in to Charisse's openly groaning mouth. He straddled her chest pushing his pipe in and out of her warm awaiting mouth. It didn't take long for him to reach climax and he pushed his large member even further down Charisse's throat as the liquid filled her mouth and ran down her cheeks. Duke didn't even want to move, he wished he could just stay there and enjoy the moment forever. But Tank had other plans. Tank took off his pants and laid on the back side of Charisse. He knew he was too large to try to enter her from the top. He held her right leg up in the air, to give his small penis a better chance of gaining entrance. The hot wet feeling of Charisse vaginal walls was complete heaven. Tank didn't think the feeling of Charisse could match her taste, but he was definitely wrong. He stroked her with small slow grinds, trying to savor the feeling of ecstasy he was now in. But the mixture of the fluid, the heat and the grabbing of her ass made Charisse's pussy muscles tighten up so much that Tank began to explode inside her. Tank let out a loud scream and moan as if he was trying to push a 500 hundred pound weight of his chest. Duke looked at the amount of sweat the large man had worked up with the little work he had just put in. He really wanted to see if Charisse's pussy matched her mouth. But after seeing Tank fat ass, nut all inside her, he figured he would wait until she had a chance to bath herself.

"Shit the bitch wasn't going anywhere any time soon." he thought to himself. Meanwhile, Tank, had started placing, first one, then two, then four fingers inside Charisse's still wet sex pot. While he was going in and out with wreck less abandonment, Charisse had placed her middle finger on her clit and was beginning to orgasm. Her body jerked with such motions, Tank sat there mesmerized by the effect he thought his fisting was doing to the young beautiful woman. Duke sat back in the chair and just observed the sick manner in which Tank continued to fondle Charisse.

"Damn getting some pussy was one thing, but Tank wasn't giving her a break." Duke thought to himself. However with the serious look on his friend's face, Duke was un-willing to step in and stop his madness. Charisse was clearly out of it and not even responding to Tanks entry into her vagina, then placing the same fingers in her ass, and finally into his mouth. Unable to stand it any longer Duke walked outside onto the porch of the aged yellow house. Just as he light up a blunt to remove the images of Tank and Charisse from his mind. A green Cadillac with gold rims pulled up. It was his counterpart who had left to take Cowboy home. Only he wasn't by himself, Hakeem was sitting on the passenger side. He wasn't quite sure how Hakeem would respond to the party that had just taken place and the one that Tank continued inside. He tried to let Tank know that Hakeem had pulled up, but he was too late. Hakeem and Rick were already exiting the car.

"What up my nigga?" Hakeem asked while reaching for the blunt.

"It ain't shit bro," Duke responded while passing it to Hakeem. Hakeem could sense the nervousness in Duke's demeanor, and quickly asked "Where Tank?"

"He inside!"

"What about the girl?"

"She inside too!" Duke promptly responded. Hakeem opened the door to see his partner lying on the couch with Charisse's naked body on top of him. He was rubbing her hair like she was a small puppy. Once Tank recognized that it was Hakeem, he threw Charisse off him and onto the floor.

"Uhh...Uhhh... me and Duke was just having a little fun with shorty, that's all Havoc, Tank blurted out.

Hakeem turned and stared at Duke who had a guilty look on his face. Both men stood like two kids who had just broke their mother's favorite dish. Hakeem finally broke the silence.

"Please tell me how you nigga's going to get at that pussy before me?"

Tank and Duke smiled simultaneously as they realized that they were both of the hook.

"Tank since your big ass over there with the bitch all laid up on you like a baby, how about you take her in the bathroom and clean her up and get her ready for a real nigga! And what you give the hoe? Cause I know the bitch got to be riding on something to let you two thirsty nigga's hit without a fight!" Hakeem turned and hit Rick in the stomach with a light tap.

Almost on queue Rick began to laugh along with Hakeem. Tank did as he was told and with meticulous detail he washed Charisse from head to toe. Hakeem and Rick got tired of waiting and came inside the small bathroom and both took turns having their way with Charisse. Duke even had a second round once Rick and Hakeem grew tired of the sex with the limp body. Once every man had fully relieved themselves, Hakeem instructed Tank to tie her back up, but leave her clothes off, just in case he got the feeling again.

Selena and Kasy pulled the black SUV into the parking space available behind the 2012 silver 535 BMW. The Target parking lot was the fifth stop Tiffany had made on the rainy night and both Selena and Kasy were growing tired of waiting for the opportunity to grab her. But they each knew that the situation required both patience and discipline. With this in mind, Target wasn't the right place, with of all the security cameras lining the department store parking area. After about an hour and half, Tiffany returned to her vehicle. She popped the trunk and placed four large bags inside. She looked around as if she knew someone was watching her, but for whatever reason she never thought to look at the vehicle right behind her. Instead she jumped into the driver's seat of her car and headed back down highway 85 South in the direction of the Westside of Charlotte. Kasy was dipping in and out of the interstate traffic in attempt to keep up with Tiffany who was driving like she was in a Nascar speed chase. Finally she exited off the expressway to West Blvd. Tiffany traveled about a mile down the road before she pulled into a small corner store. Kasy perked up as he instructed Selena to get ready.

"Look cuzzo this is as good as it probably is going to get, you know this small ass store don't have no outside security. So once she comes back out go ahead and grab the bitch so we can get back to our side of town."

Selena, as if she didn't need the pep talk, was already half way out the car before Kasy finished. As Tiffany was about to re-enter her vehicle, she felt the pinch of the cold steel of the pistol at her lower back and mid-section.

"Bitch just give me a reason to finish that ass whopping I started on you at the club," Selena whispered into her ear.

Tiffany just froze, the ice cold Snapple bottle she was sipping on, began to shake vigorously in her hand. While Selena walked her back to the 2012 Chevy Tao, She placed Tiffany into the front seat and entered the rear taking the seat directly behind Tiffany.

Kasy shot Tiffany a smile and offered her some kind words. "Look ma, just do as you're told and you can be home by to tomorrow. But, if you or your man decides to act up...... Well let's just say neither of you will see home again, you understand?"

Tiffany shook her head, letting Kasy know that she understood fully.

"See cuz isn't it beautiful when everyone can get along." Kasy said in a joking manner, looking back to Selena who still had the gun barrel fixed on Tiffany's head. Kasy pulled out his cell phone and scrolled down to Brianna's name and pressed send.

She quickly answered "Yes! Tell me something good, please!"

"We got the package and headed back to the spot, so make the call and we can get this shit over with tonight" Kasy spoke.

"No doubt, I'll hit you back once I let this nigga know two can play this game." Brianna responded with a smile on her face. She hadn't showing any signs of pleasure in the last week. But she was sure that would be over once she called Hakeem and let him know that she had his baby's mother and would only be willing to allow her to see tomorrow if he was prepared to trade Charisse's life for Tiffany's. Brianna quickly ended the call with Kasy and press Charisse's number since it was the last number the kidnappers had called her from. She made sure to push facetime. Brianna wanted to see the expression on Hakeem face when she gave him the bad news. Just as she had expected, Hakeem answered the phone on the third ring. He was standing in the living room of the small house with Rick and Duke. So he quickly pressed the speaker icon so his boys could hear Brianna beg him for her sister's life.

"What it do bitch, you got my bread ready?" Hakeem asked in a smug tone. Rick and Duke smiled at the boss way Hakeem was handling Brianna.

"Bitch? ...Nigga, I know you ain't talking with your snitch ass. I heard what happen to you up in county with your weak punk self. You telling that hoe of a baby momma of yours that I was just sucking your dick, but the word out here is my head ain't shit compared to yours!" Brianna let out a small chuckle.

Hakeem sat on the phone in complete silence for a moment. Although he knew it wasn't true, the fact that Brianna said some shit like that had him steaming. Then to add insult to injury, his partners were looking at him with a faces that asked "Is this true?" Hakeem knew no matter what he said it wouldn't 100% clear his boy's minds.

"Bitch you still there? Brianna asked feeling that her words had cut him deep. She continued "And pussy boy, there won't be no money exchange instead it will be a life for a life. Yea bitch ass nigga I got your girl and if you want to see her again, how about you listen up and let me tell you how this shit is going to go down." Brianna smiled inwardly feeling like she posed the upper hand.

"You stupid yellow bitch! You think I give a fuck about that hoe? Shit I got three more baby momma's, I will lose that one gladly. Now are you ready to lose your sister is the question. From what I remember you don't have too many people who love you in this world. So you tell me bitch what life you exchanging me for her, because the only ones I'm interested in is the dead lives of presidents on that green paper. And since you want to be so cute and fly with the mouth and you think a nigga playing with you. How about I show you this shit is real!"

"Go get that bitch!" Hakeem shouted to Duke and Rick, "and bring her pretty ass in here so I can show her sister what we do to bitches with fly mouths!"

Brianna couldn't make out what happened because the screen kept going in and out of focus from the constant movement. Once the movement stopped the picture came back into focus and Brianna could see Hakeem's face with two men holding Charisse behind him. Charrise had been stripped down to nothing but her panties and bra.

Brianna yelled into the phone "Hakeem I know you a dirty nigga, but please tell me you didn't allow them bastards to violate my sister?" Brianna asked with a shiver in her voice and her eyes filling up with tears.

"Hell no I didn't just let them violate her, I got me some of that Campbell pussy too, and I got to say that shit was good, but she ain't got you babe, so don't worry, you still my GOAT. Brianna began shaking her head vigorously from side to side.

Through clinched teeth Brianna issued another threat. "Hakeem I'm going to give you this money and then I'm going to kill you, do you understand that?"

Hakeem laughed loudly, starting a ripple effect with the other two men around him. Almost on cue they all stop when Hakeem began to speak again. "Brianna babe, I'm not through with you or her yet. So if that got you ready to kill a nigga, I got something really good for you." Hakeem turned around and spoke to his two goons, "Take that tape off that little bitch's mouth."

Duke did as he was instructed and Charisse screamed, "Bri help me please sis help me please......." She was cut off by a viscous right hook from Hakeem to the jaw. Charisse felt the pain all through her skull, but before she could cry out another blow caught the other side of her face. She wanted to cry but the constant barrage of punches drove her small frame to the floor. Where she was met with kicks and stomps from all three men. Hakeem made sure he kept the phone's camera directly on the damage him and his boys were putting in on Charisse. Finally once Charisse's body went limp he yelled back into the phone, "Now Bitch do you still think I'm playing with your stanking ass?"

Brianna couldn't even speak, she just nodded her head in agreement.

"Good, now to make sure you fully understand, and so that we don't have any more mix ups. Plus that little comment earlier, this is for you." Hakeem walked over to Charisse he grabbed her still motionless frame and placed it before the dirty toilet in the small bathroom. He opened her mouth and positioned it on the dirty rim of the porcelain area. Charisse's head kept tilting to the side. So Hakeem had Rick come over and hold it up right, like I place kicker on the football field.

Brianna screamed with horror coating her every word "Please Hakeem don't do this!" she begged, "I understand... I didn't mean to say that, I'm sorry...please Hakeem I will give you whatever you want please... please....."

Brianna's cries went unanswered has Hakeem took his booted right foot and with all the force of his torso he smashed the heel of his shoe into the back of Charisse's head. The force of the impact made aloud thump, only to be followed by the cracking of Charisse's teeth against the strong porcelain structure.

Duke turned his head; the Bojangles he had consumed earlier was about to come back up. "Damn," he thought to himself, "Hakeem is one sick mother fucker".

Rick let Charisse's head fall to the floor. Blood was gushing from her mouth and nose.

Hakeem looked back into the phone, "Now have my money here before midnight, you come alone and if I even think you got someone with you, I will put your sister out her misery!" Hakeem lifted up Charisse's head to get a good look at the damage he had inflicted. Then continued "You may want to make it before eleven I don't want the little bitch to bleed out," he said with a laugh. The screen went blank.

****

Brianna's whole body began to tremble; she knew that all this was her fault. She started to think that maybe her step father had been right. It seemed like everything she touched ended up in a worse position because of her. But she knew she had no time to soak in her own misery, Charisse needed her more now than ever. Brianna took several deep breaths and on the last one she held it as long as possible before blowing all the old wind out of her lungs.

She called Kasy's phone and in a slow monotone voice she spoke, "Kasy the plan is off, Hakeem don't give a fuck about that chick or nobody else, I'm going to have to pay him the money to get my sister back, and that's how it's going to be."

"But Bri....." Kasy tried to interject.

Brianna cut him off in her same tone, "No Kasy there are no buts, I have to follow what he says. I don't give fuck about this money or what happens to me anymore. I have lost the love of my life because of money and I'm not about to lose the one other person who loves me in this world for the same reason."

Kasy could hear the defeat in her voice so he didn't try to convince her that going alone was a bad decision. Instead he offered some common street reasoning. "Look Bri, you the boss and I really feel your pain. But if you not going to let us go with you, at least text me the address once you get there. That way if the nigga decide to try some funny shit, you can go knowing that me and Selena got your back, you feel me mama?"

"Yea, I feel you, so that's a fo sure." Brianna had to admit that would be a great last thought, knowing that Hakeem and his crew would never live to enjoy the money. Kasy I love you and tell Selena I love her too."

"Na ma you going to have to tell her yourself when we meet after this shit is over, and I love you too."

Brianna hung up the phone and went into her small office and removed the large Persian rug from the middle of the floor, revealing the in-floor safe. With shaking hands she punched in the code to the digital pad 12-20-75, Tre's birthday. The green light and the clicking sound signaled that the safe was ready to be opened. Brianna counted out the half million dollars and placed it into the two large Louis Vuitton luggage carriers. Her phone began to ring again and she looked down at the screen to see Brandon's name and picture smiling up at her. Seeing his expression put a large grin on her face. But she swiftly pressed ignored. He had been calling her for that last 3 days and she had been ignoring him every time, waiting for the drama in her life to be over so she could spend some quality time with him. But the way her life was going the drama would never end and in her mind Brianna felt that it would be better to let Brandon go on his way before he got wrapped up in her deadly world.

Brianna placed the suit cases in her Range Rover and prepared to leave. As she pulled out the driveway she saw Brandon trying to flag her down out the corner of her eye. Knowing she was in no state of mind to talk with him. She pressed harder on the accelerator and ignored his cries as the truck drove down the narrow dark street. Until Brandon could only see the brakes light as Brianna made a right onto the major street.

****

Cowboy and Tank pulled up a block away from the brick front home, where they had begun there latest mission. Only this time they were going to get Herman. Herman didn't know that when he made his deal with Hakeem, he had made a pact with the devil.

It was Cowboy's second visit to the house in less than a week. The feeling he had received earlier was coming back to him. He knew that he knew the street and the home whose driveway they sat quietly in. Tank broke Cowboy's thought's as his mind began to trace back through his mind attempting to match up his location with the memory.

"Yo unk, remember everyone inside must die, no one left breathing is how Keem wants it, you feel me?"

"Yea I got you young blood, but one question, why we got to bring the bodies back? That's like throwing rocks at the penitentiary, riding around with dead bodies in the car. Does your man not trust that we handling our business?"

"Unk I don't know, but for a hundred fifty stacks I don't give a fuck. If you want, you don't have to ride back with me and the bodies and we can split the money 70/30." Tank said with a sly smile on his face. Cowboy looked back over at him with a nigga please look before he responded. "Youngin just get out the car and lets go take care of this shit, so I can get my money."

"Yea that's what I figured." Tank responded while opening the door to the sedan and heading to the rear of the house.

The entire yard was still as dark as the night when they had come to kidnap Charisse. The only difference was a TV was clearly on and loudly blasting some type of sports game. Tank opened the small fenced door that led to the rear patio of the home. When he stepped on the old wooded deck, he thought he had given himself and his partner away with the loud creeks resounding from the dying wood with every step he and Cowboy took looking through the glass patio doors that were absent of any curtains. They could see Herman laid out on the sofa with nearly an empty fifth of Kentucky liquor bottle hanging from his left hand. There was also Budweiser beer cans scattered on the coffee table in front of him.

"This should be easier than we thought Unk, this nigga is dead drunk and knocked the fuck out, should we kill him here or take him with us?

"No need in waiting to kill the poor sap, let's take him out and get the fuck outta here before someone comes." The two men carefully opened the sliding door and stepped inside.

Cowboy pulled out his buck knife signaling to Tank that he would cut their victim's throat, but Tank waved him off and whispered, "Keem said two shots to the head and bring the murder weapon and the body back.

Cowboy was really getting pissed off at all the direction that he had to follow in taking this man's life, but he knew that these kind of hundred and fifty thousand dollar come ups had come few and far between in his late age. So he followed instruction and reached into the small of his back for the gun to finish the job. Just has he removed the weapon, he and Tank both heard the front door opening. They quickly searched the room for a place to hide, so they could take their second victim by surprise. Cowboy chose a narrow entry way into the hall and Tank got tightly up against the wall beside the entrance into the living room.

Lorraine laid her keys down on the kitchen table; she could hear the TV blasting through the front door when she came inside. She assumed Herman was the culprit behind all of the clamor in their home. But she wasn't about to complain, especially since he had given her $500 hundred dollars to go play the poker machines and she had turned that $500 into $1200. She was feeling real good, until she step into the room where all the noise and her husband was. Lorraine was suddenly greeted by a large black figure with a gun pointed to the side of her head. Cowboy stood motionless as he looked at Lorraine's face. All the history that his mind was trying to recall began playing back in a second. He knew exactly where he was and who she was. He looked at the scared look on her face and then at the deadly look on Tank face. Just as Tank was about to pull the trigger, Cowboy raised his gun and fired four shots. The first one caught Tank in the arm that was holding the pistol. The second and third pierced his chest swinging him around until the final head shoot put him to rest forever.

Lorrain was screaming uncontrollably as Cowboy tried to comfort her and move her away from Tanks death body. All the commotion hadn't awaken Herman from his drunken slumber.

"Joe.... what are you doing in my house....... and who is this man you just killed?" Lorrain asked while tears rolled down her cheeks.

Cowboy looked her over as he held her close to him. She was still as beautiful as the first time he met her so many years ago. Then his mind clicked again "If this was Lorraine's house then where was his daughter? Oh no," he wondered to himself, "could the girl back at the house be his one and only child. And had he allowed these men to violate her?" Cowboy began to scan the walls looking for a photo of the girl he and Tank had kidnapped. He saw a younger version of the female on the wall and quickly grabbed the picture.

"Lorraine is this our child is this Brianna?" He asked, scared as hell of the answer. "Is this our daughter??" He yelled even louder

"No it's not Brianna, that's my daughter Charisse." Cowboy didn't know if he should believe her so he asked her to show him a picture of Brianna. Lorrain simply looked down at the request.

"Lorraine please let me see what she looks like," Cowboy begged.

"Joe..... we don't have any pictures of Brianna in this house, my husband won't allow it." She answered while pointing at Herman. Cowboy looked at her with a confused look in his eyes, but realized that Lorraine would have to do the explaining on their way back to house where Charisse was held up. He knew he needed to get back there and fast.

****

Hakeem grabbed a blunt and his cell phone and walked out onto the porch of the small house. Before he closed the door he gave Duke and Rick some quick instructions.

"Look you'll keep your eyes on girlie and do something to stop that bleeding. We can't have our meal ticket die before the pay out, you feel me. "He shut door and unlocked his cell phone. Hakeem took a long swig on the fat blunt, then exhaled deeply in time to start his conversation with the man on the other end of the phone.

"Hakeem, what it is my friend" the older white gentleman asked.

Hakeem sucked his teeth in disgust at how officer Woods always tried to act like they were friends or when they spoke. Hakeem knew he was just another nigga that the feds were using to lock up other niggas. But this was the road he had chosen for himself, so he dealt with it.

"Yea whatever, I'm just calling to let you know, that what I promised is about to be delivered. Give me three hours and come to the location I just texted to your phone."

"And you're saying that I will get Mrs. Campbell, a dead body, her prints on the weapon, and drug money, correct?"

"Yes Sir, and I'm throwing in 2 kilos of crack, to seal your case and her fate," Hakeem added.

"Hakeem my man, see, aren't you glad you're on my team, now you will be the head nigga on the streets of Charlotte..... Well as long as you cooperate with me that is.

Hakeem looked at the phone," this cracker just called me nigga, he thought to himself," he was about to respond, however his better judgment kicked in and he hung the phone up and released a big smile. His plan was coming all together. Not only would he get his revenge on Brianna, by sentence her to the life she had planned for him. But he would also get a cool 250 thousand after he gave the others their cut of the half million. And with Brianna gone he would have all the trap houses in Charlotte on lock. Hakeem turned and went back inside the house to get prepared for Brianna, who would arrive in a little over an hour.

"Ok boy's let's go over this one more time. Tank and Cowboy should be getting back here with the old man shortly. I'm thinking we're going to have to kill lil sis there too. But we will wait until after Bri shows us the money..."

"You sure shawty going to bring all that bread and no muscle with her Keem?" Duke asked cutting Hakeem off.

"Yea nigga I'm sure, That's why I went so hard on the phone with the bitch. I had to let her know we wasn't bullshiting. Plus that bitch sitting on a lot of paper, so this half a mill ain't shit to her!"

"Well damn if that's the case, why you didn't ask for more?" Rick chimed in.

"See my nigga, that's why you not in charge," Hakeem responded while shaking his head. "If we would have asked for more, sure enough she would have gave it, but she would have been going into her connects pocket to do so. And with the amount of dope she supplying, that's a pretty big connect. So that should let you know them nigga's major and we don't want no problems with nigga's like that, you feel me? It's like what Frank White say in "Scarface" you don't want to be too big or to small fly low and you can fly forever..."

Hakeem heard Charisse's phone ring again. Duke tossed the phone over to him and Hakeem saw that it was Brianna.

"See nigga's that's my babe, right on time." He pressed the accept button "Bri tell me something good."

"I have your money and I'm in the car, so where am I coming to?" she asked in a cold tone.

"Well I know you got GPS in whatever you driving, so just punch in 5585 Central ave, and call me when you outside. Oh and Bri remember what I said you come alone or you will be taking your sister back in a body bag, you got me?"

"I got you Hakeem, all I want is my sister back, I don't care about this money."

"Now isn't that love, well just keep in mind bitch it's about the money for me, so don't try no stupid shit." Hakeem hung the phone up before she could say anything back. He could hear the grief in Brianna's voice and he loved it.

****

Brianna entered the address into the GPS as Hakeem had suggested. The navigation system informed her that the estimated arrival time was 45 min away, which meant that she had 30 minutes to put together a plan. She knew that there was no way Hakeem was letting her and Charisse walk away alive. Brianna had a quick flashback to the night Tre was killed. She fully understood why Tre wouldn't give up the location of the money or the dope. He knew that they were going to kill him anyway. She prayed out loud asking Tre and God to give her and Charisse protection and to send her an idea. But 40 minutes later there was still nothing she could think of. As she drove down the long, dark gravel road. She could see the small yellow house coming into view.

Her thoughts was interrupted by a loud white woman's voice "You have arrived 5585 Central Ave. Your destination is on the right." Her GPS had confirmed that she was out of time. Brianna reached down and called the last number back.

"I seen you pull up, now roll all the window's down and open the doors, my men are going to come out and make sure you alone." Hakeem spoke into the phone.

Brianna did as she was told as Duke and Rick came out the house to check out the vehicle. Brianna kept her eyes on them as both men walked around her truck with guns drawn. Brianna took the phone and switched it to her left hand and took her right hand and placed it on the butt of her pistol she had in her purse. She gently released the safety, if they thought she was going out without a fight they would be sadly mistaken. The two men waved to Hakeem who was standing in the window signaling that everything was clear.

"Ok good, I see you still know how to follow direction. So now give them the money and once they bring it inside I will bring out Charisse." Hakeem suggested.

"No way I'm sending this money in without, seeing my sister first. Brianna interjected.

"Ok babe have it your way, you bring the money inside then and we can make the exchange"

"Hakeem do you think I'm stupid? There's no way I'm coming inside there, you bring her out and put her in the truck and take your money out at the same time."

"So you think I'm stupid then? Fuck that we will meet in the middle!"

"What's the middle?" Brianna asked.

"The porch bitch!" Hakeem laughed back. Hakeem really didn't care where the deal went down. He was just trying to buy sometime for Tank and Cowboy to get back with Herman's dead body so everything would be in place for agent woods.

"Well you know I got's to count that money before you get lil sis right? I remember how you use to hate counting money. So you may have not counted it right."

"Whatever Hakeem, let's just get this shit over with!" Brianna was growing tired of Hakeem's cat and mouse game. She pulled off her seat belt and slid her gun into the waist line of the seven jeans she had on. The leather jacket she had on concealed the weapon from Duke and Rick. She popped open the rear door of the truck and walked around to pull out the contents. She stopped as she drug both suit cases out and onto the ground.

"Damn you nigga's just going to watch me try to carry this shit? You know they not going to roll on this gravel, can a bitch get some help?" Both men looked into the direction of Hakeem to get approval before assistant Brianna. Hakeem who was standing on the front porch nodding his head in consent.

"Damn Bri you sure looking good in those jeans babe. You know a nigga miss that good loving you use to give, right. So tell me is there someone new knocking the bottom out that pussy, the way I use too?"

"Don't flatter yourself Hakeem, you wasn't all that, and I don't know about you touching the bottom of anything. You must got me and Tiffany mixed up." Brianna responded stopping the laughs of Rick and Duke from Hakeem's earlier statement.

"Well Bri you remember your way and I will remember it mine. I just hate it had to come to this. You know we made a good team and couple. And you had to let a little thing like me killing a nigga get in the way."

"Well that nigga was my man and you're suppose it best friend, remember!"

"Yea, yea, yea, but just like you he didn't understand that when Hakeem need something, it's best just to give it to him, or you force me to take it and someone dies in the process ."

"Fuck all the small talk Hakeem, where is my sister?"

"Oh so you grew a set of ball back since the last time daddy had to straighten you. Don't make me do a repeat on your pretty ass up in here."

"Hakeem I'm ready to die and take you and these sorry ass nigga's with me. So if that's what you want let's do it!" Brianna said with a look of death on her face.

"Na...na babe I got some money to spend and some more living to do. Beside's I don't want to see you dead. In fact I got a surprise for you, for old time sakes. "

"The only thing I need from you is my sister, now where is she at?"

Hakeem motioned for Brianna to join him in the house to retrieve Charisse. This time Brianna didn't oppose entry into the home. Once inside Hakeem told Duke to go bring Charisse from the bathroom. Hakeem saw a set of head lights shine into the small house. "Good,"he thought to himself, "that must be Tank and Cowboy with the old man." They were right on time.

"Rick, go outside and help Tank and Cowboy and give me and my lady some time alone." Rick did followed his instructions. Hakeem approached Brianna with both of his hands up signaling that he was unarmed.

"Like I was saying Bri, I really missed you," he got up closer to where he could smell the scent of the soap she used on her skin. "Damn and you still smell so good." Hakeem continued while bending down and rubbing his nose across her neck. He took his hands down to Brianna's zipper and gently pulled it down. Brianna stood there motionless, she was hoping that she could catch him off guard and draw her gun from her waist. So she allowed him to play is little game. Hakeem placed two of his fingers into Brianna's pants he could feel the soft material of her Victoria Secret's panties. He maneuvered them to the side and placed his large middle finger into Brianna's dry pussy. He felt around hoping that it would get wet, but her body wouldn't respond to his vicious assault. He pulled out the finger and placed it into his mouth. Just as he was about to speak, Brianna pulled the gun and placed it in his face.

"Now nigga, I hope you enjoyed that because it's the last pussy you ever going to taste!" Now get down on your knees." Hakeem did as he was told, while holding both hands up.

"Bri are you stupid or do you think I'm stupid. You know my boys on their way back in here and even if you kill me. It's no way you and Charisse walking up out here. So just put the gun down and once we leave you can take Charisse home and live to fight another day. You smarter....."

"Boom...Boom...Boom" Hakeem and Brianna could hear the

loud sounds of gun fire coming from outside. The loud boom had caused Brianna to look towards the open door giving Hakeem a quick second to make a run to an open entry to the kitchen. But not before Brianna got off two shoots of her own catching him in the shoulder and chest. Brianna turned her weapon to the door of the house ready to shoot whoever came through first. Just as the old man entered the house Brianna's was about to fire, when directly behind him she saw a familiar face, Lorrain.

"Baby don't shoot!" Lorrain yelled.

"Momma what are you doing here, and who is he?" Brianna asked confused.

"We don't have time for that right now baby, we got to get you and your sister outta here quickly" Cowboy uttered.

"Nigga I'm not going nowhere with you, until you let me know who the fuck you are and what you're doing with my......." Brianna was interrupted by the opening of the bathroom door. It was Duke and he had Charisse in front of him with a gun to her head.

"Cowboy where is Hakeem and Rick?" Duke asked in a frantic voice.

"Rick is outside and Hakeem is out there with him." Cowboy responded.

"Well what the fuck was all that shooting for?"

"Boy the girl got off two shots, but she didn't hit shit, Hakeem made it outside and sent me in here. Cowboy turned to Brianna winked his eye and continued."Now young lady like I was telling you just drop the gun and no one will get hurt."

Brianna looked at Cowboy like he was crazy. Lorrain's friend or not it was no way she putting down the gun. Cowboy must have read her mind so he made his way towards Duke and Charisse.

"Well boy since she not going to put the gun down give me the girl and go see what Hakeem want us to do."

"Nigga why don't you go see?" Duke asked

"Because boy you know you ain't never killed nobody, now give me the girl!"

Just as Duke moved away from Charisse, Cowboy place the gun to his head and fired. All the contents of his skull splattered onto the nearby wall and onto Charisse's skin. Cowboy placed the hot

126

weapon onto the TV as he held Charisse up.

"Nigga I don't know who you are but get your fucking hands off my sister" Brianna shouted while pointing the gun in his direction."

Lorraine quickly shouted. "Brianna he is.....he's your father..... This is your daddy baby."

"What? "Brianna asked unsure how to digest this sudden revelation. "What do you mean my father, I don't have a father." She stated coldly.

"Brianna I know this is a lot to take in right now, and you have a lot of questions, but this is not the time or the place. We really got to get out here befor............"

Pow..Pow..Pow Cowboy couldn't finish his statement, he felt the burning sensations of the hot melt entering his chest. He could feel his legs losing the strength to hold his body. He had been shot before so he knew this feeling all too well. He turned to see Hakeem crawling on the floor with a shot gun in his hand. Cowboy tried to fire back but couldn't hit his target from the fetal position he was now in.

Brianna walked over behind Hakeem and fired a shot into his back. The force of the bullet knock the sawed off gun from Hakeem's hand. Brianna took her full leather boot and rolled Hakeem over so she could see his face.

"Nigga I want you to look at me before I kill you!"

Hakeem just smiled, he knew even in death he would get Brianna back, it wouldn't long before agent woods would be there, and even though Rick, Duke and his own body's were not what he promised agent wood's he knew that they would do.

"Go ahead bitch kill me, you going to have a long time to think about it!" Hakeem said while spitting out a gob of blood and continued. "Yea I got your red ass, I got the Feds on the way here now and with the money, the dope I got planet and the dead bodies. You going to be thinking about ole Keem for a long time where you going. So go ahead Bri, I'll be sure to tell Tre hey when I get there!"

"Nigga you won't be seeing my baby, where you going!" Brianna pressed firmly on the trigger as she put two shots into Hakeem's head making sure that he was dead. "

Brianna ran over to Charisse, she was still bleeding and very disoriented. She picked her up and placed her on the sofa. She then walked over to Cowboy who was now cupped in Lorraine's arms.

"How you doing?" she asked looking down onto his face, a face that she saw all of herself in.

"I'll live baby, but you got to get your mother and sister outta here before the Feds get here.

"No you'll need to get outta here, its' no need for me to run, that snitch nigga already set me up so even if I run once they get here and see this mess, they coming to my front door. I might as well get the shit over with now."

"Baby like I said, get your sister and mother and go. I know I have never been a father to you before, and I sure as hell have never did anything for you. So please let me do this, you got so much more living to do."

At that moment it dawned on Brianna what Cowboy was suggesting. This was the father she always wanted, but why did they have to meet under these circumstances? That had been the story of her life. Right man, wrong time. She wasn't about to look the protection she had prayed for from Tre and God in the face and deny its help. She leaned down and kissed him on his cheek and hugged him tightly.

"Thank you da...." Brianna wanted desperately to call him daddy, but neither her mouth or heart would let her finish the sentence. Instead she simply smiled, "Come on mom let's get Charisse and get outta here.

Lorrain and Brianna loaded Charrise into the car. Brianna went back into the house and helped Cowboy onto the couch, she found a small blanket in one of the rooms and placed it over him. She then dragged both suit case back out to her truck and loaded them inside.

She got into the car and pulled away from the house. Mere minutes later, as she turned onto the four lane expressway, she could see the unmarked cars with the blue lights flashing on their way to the house. Wouldn't they be surprise to find she wasn't there and their star snitch dead.

****

Seeing Herman at the hospital had Brianna's blood boiling. "Here this nigga is acting like he didn't have nothing to do with this shit" she thought to herself. After Lorraine had told her everything Cowboy shared with her on the ride to Hakeem's hide out. They both thought is was best to not share the info with Charisse, who both felt had been through enough. Brianna sternly walked up to Herman and whispered in his ear

"Let me see you outside for a minute" she spoke in a direct order kinda way. Herman looked at her as if she was crazy.

"we don't have anything to speak about" he shot back and turned back facing Charisse.

"well maybe you want me to call the police and let them know who setup the kidnapping that led to your daughter lying in this hospital bed." Brianna whispered now leaning even closer to Herman's ear. The look on his face was the same as a person who had just seen a ghost. This time Brianna didn't even wait for a response she was already out the door walking towards the family waiting room. When she finally turned around there was Herman stand there looking like a 5 year old who had just been found out. Still he tried to deny his involvement.

"I don't know what you think you know, but whatever it is you are wrong." He quickly started the conversation off with.

"Look Herman, I already know everything, so you can cut the bull shit. the only reason why you still alive, is because of my sister and the fact that she love you. Even though you don't deserve her love. I won't share that fact that her own father handing her over to men who violated her and almost took her life....."

"Look I had no idea they was going to do that, they said they was not going to hurt her, it was suppose to be you!"

"Damn what did I ever do to you to make you hate me so much. You know what it doesn't even mat...."

"You were born!" Herman cut her off saying

"Wow, I guess thats what I get for even asking a sorry nigga like you" Brianna uttered back

"But for now on we don't even have to pretend that's it's any love lost. SO let me tell you now, how this is going to work. First thing is I know my mom told you about the man that was killed in your house. While your ass was to drunk to know what was happen. Well do you know where that dead body is? I'll tell you, I had some of my associates to bury him in your back yard. I also had them put the murder weapon in your hands, so guess who prints are all over it. and who do you think now has the possession of the gun. Briann pointed to herself, while Herman stood there with a dumb found look on his face.

"So the next time you think about asking Charisse for some money, don't! The next time you think you want to threaten to call the feds on me don't! Because if you do, I will make sure that someone lets the police know where the body and the murder weapon is. Do you understand me? Herman looked down at the floor and shook his head yes. No I want to hear you say "yes Brianna I understand"

"Yes Brianna I understand" Herman spoke in a low sobering voice.

"Good, now you can leave" Brianna watched him walk away. It was all she could do to not have Kasy really teach him a lesson. but she knew he was already dying slowly and that was enough for her. She looked at her watch and realize that she had to leave now to make her next stop on time.

****

Breanna anxiously awaited behind the 3 inch thick glass window. Her mind frantically race back and Forth replaying the events of the past week. Looking around the ghostly tomb like surroundings gave her insides the same chills that her outter body was experiencing." damn must they have this place so cold" she thought out loud. Breanna was also still trying to come to grips with the fact of how close she had come to be in these same inhumane conditions, possibly for life. It was no telling what kind of sentence a triple homicide, along with drugs and cash would have produce for her. The light tap on the thick glass snapped her back to the present. The bright orange jumpsuit sagged loosely on the man's steel large frame. His eyes though hard, bore a sensitive resolve that maid Breanna feel safe. He gave her a slight smile before reaching for the small phone which served as their only line of communication. Brianna followed his lead and place the phone to her ear. She didn't know what to say, part of her wanted to thank him so much for what he had done. But the other part wanted to cuss him out and tell him how much she didn't need or want him in her life. She had rehearsed the latter feeling so many times over the years. It was what had allowed her to survive, the thought of knowing that since he didn't want to know or love her, she didn't want to know or love him. anger began to fill her heart and her eyes began to water. Cowboy could sense the emotion beginning to build and after a few moments he finally broke the icy silence

"Hey how is your sister doing?"

"She's fine, thanks for asking" Brianna responded wiping the small tears from her eyes.

" what brings you down here" Cowboy asked trying to make light conversation.

" I came to see if you needed anything.........Brianna shook her head, then after a small pause, she continued, "no I'm lying I came to ask you why?

"Why?" Cowboy looked confused

"Why did you never love me, why did you never want to see me, talk to me, hold me in your arms and be a father to me! Why was I not worth it?? Brianna was now not able to hold back the 20 something years of pain and tears. Cowboy tried to hold a stern face, at that moment he would have rather faced the judge prepared to give him the death penalty, then to look into his little girls eyes and try to answer a question he knew it wasn't a proper answer too. What reason could a man have for abandon his own flesh and blood. There was none but he had to let her know it wasn't her it was his on insecurities. He knew he had to lift the weight off her heart.

"Brianna sweetie, I so love and loved you, I was young and stupid, but beyond that I was selfish. I wanted to come get you and be a father to you. But look at me all my life Ive been a criminal, I have committed nearly every crime on the book. What kind of father could I have been to you. Every time I got in the car and was coming to pick you up. I would turn into your mother and step-father's neoborhood and I would see those nice homes, with their well manicured lawns. and I would say to myself what are you doing, you can't compete with this. What was I going to do bring you back to the one bedroom place I had in the projects? Here your step-father was a big time business man who owned his own restaurants. and here i was this common thief and hustler with nothing to show or give you. I would see you out side on the porch of that beautiful home with that nice car in the drive way. and I had nothing to offer you."

"Love" Brianna screamed into the phone.

"Huh"

"love, you could have offered me love, something I so desperately wanted and need it." Cowboy wasn't expecting that, in his mind he could justify his action, knowing that he had nothing, but she had one upped him with the one thing he did have for her. He was now unable to hold back tears that was streaming down his cheeks.

"I'm sorry Brianna, I didn't think my love was worthy of wanting. I made a mistake I will have to live with for the rest of my life. But I don't want you to carry this weight any longer. You deserve a life filled with love and all that God as to offer to you. You hear me? it was never you it was always me and I hope that one day you can forgive me for it. If you will have me I would like to have a chance to get to know you. Brianna wanted to guard her feelings, she wanted to make him hurt longer like she had. But her heart wouldn't let her. She looked into his face and it was like looking into a mirror. All that time she thought she looked like her mother, but now it was clear that her father had spit her out. She wished that the glass was not in-between them, she so wanted to reach out and feel his arms around her. She needed his love as if she was still 7 years old.

"Brianna can we start over?" he asked in a low tone

"No.... we can't start over!" Brianna screamed, the words made Cowboy dropped his head.

" but we can start from here and work I'll way forwarded... agreed?" Brianna smiled

he lifted his head back up "Agreed" Cowboy smiled back.

"Ok now let's wipe these tears off our faces, I don't want these young boys thinking my daddy soft and trying you back there." Brianna said in a jokingly manner.

cowboy laughed "They anit crazy, I may be old, but my name still ring out in them streets and behind this wall. Beside now they know who my daughter is, so they know better!" Brianna smiled at his usage of the word daughter, she loved it. She wanted to sit and relive 28 years at that moment. But the visiting time was up. she let him know that she would be back next week at the same time and to call if he needed anything. As she was about to leave the parking lot she heard a loud thumb in the back of the truck. She pulled over to the side of the parking deck to see what the noise was. Brianna popped the hatch to see the two suit cases of money, still lying in the truck.

"Thank You Tre" she spoke has the idea appeared in her head. She pulled the vehicle back into one of the parking spaces. She took one of the suit cases and wheeled it down to her attorneys office that sat across the street from the county jail. Just as she was entering the building she saw Attorney Conseula

"Hi Mrs. Campbell, what brings you down here today?

"I need you help" Brianna responded

"I know the federal prosecutors have not been bothering you again have they?"

"No not for me, I need you to defend my father" Brianna loved the sound of that, she now had a father!! The end..............

Please Be Sure To Check Out These Other Titles From Blake Karrington As Well.

@BlakeKarrington

Blake Karrington

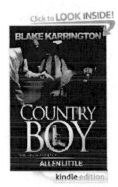
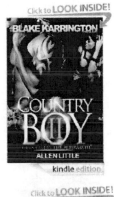

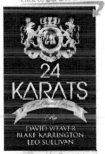

CPSIA information can be obtained at www.ICGtesting.com
Printed in the USA
LVOW09s1147261014

410555LV00001B/225/P